THE BOOK OF TIME

THE
BOOK
OF
TIME

GUILLAUME PRÉVOST

Translated by
WILLIAM RODARMOR

SCHOLASTIC INC.

New York Toronto London Auckland Sydney
Mexico City New Delhi Hong Kong Buenos Aires

For Charles and Pauline
— G. P.

Arthur A. Levine Books hardcover edition designed by Elizabeth B. Parisi, published by Arthur A. Levine Books, an imprint of Scholastic Inc., September 2007.

ISBN-13: 978-0-439-88379-5
ISBN-10: 0-439-88379-2

12 11 10 9 8 7 6 5 4 3 2 1   8 9 10 11 12 13/0

Printed in the U.S.A.   40
First Scholastic paperback printing, July 2008

CONTENTS

Sam 1

The Stone Statue 8

Iona 17

Colm Cille's Treasure 28

At the Front Lines 40

Alone in the Dark 52

The Million-Year Palace 62

The Glass Scarab 71

A Family Meeting 85

Press Review 96

A New Departure 111

The Image-Makers' Guild 125

The Hamsters of Bruges 139

Van Eyck's Secret 148

Three Livres and Twelve Sols 161

The Alchemist 174

Latin Translation 183

Surprise 195

Hansoku-Make 205

CHAPTER ONE

Sam

Samuel Faulkner's trouble with time started at 9:48 Saturday morning.

"Sammy! Saaammy!"

His grandmother's voice, calling him from downstairs.

"Is everything all right? Aren't you going to your tournament?"

Sam's eyes snapped open. *The tournament!*

"If you don't hurry, you'll miss your bus!"

The bus came at 10:06. Sam threw himself out of bed. It was his birthday, and he'd thought he could sleep in — he'd completely forgotten about the tournament! He raced around his room, pulling on a T-shirt and jeans, sweeping up his gym bag, his judo uniform, his brown belt. The tournament, where he'd be facing Monk . . .

"Sammy, what are you doing? It's almost ten o'clock."

"It's okay, Grandma. I'm coming down," he shouted back. In the room next door, a hysterical girl singer wailed on and on about a good-looking boy she just met at the beach:

He's so cute,
He's so sweet.
He makes my heart skip a beat.
Oh yes, the boy on the beeeaach!

The source of this racket would be his twelve-year-old cousin, Lily, who gathered her friends every Saturday morning for long gossip sessions with lots of stupid pop music. Amazing how he slept through noise like that!

I hope he's not out of reach.
Oh yes, the boy on the beach!

"Sammy, it's after ten o'clock!"

Sam slipped on his sneakers without tying them and looked around the room to be sure he had everything. His bus pass lay on the desk next to a framed photograph of his parents and Alicia at Thanksgiving. He gave the picture the briefest glance as he grabbed the pass, then opened the door.

As luck would have it, Lily and her little gang had taken over the hallway. They stood like a sort of honor guard for him, with mocking smiles and pastel tank tops that barely covered their stomachs.

"Did you remember the Band-Aids, Sammy?" Lily asked with fake concern. "And some ointment? We don't want you to hurt yourself, darling. Remember last year?" Last year, Sam had been crushed in forty-three seconds under Monk's fat stomach — a very bad memory. "Try to get through the first round *at least*," she added, laughing so hard she had to hold her sides. "After all, you never know!"

"Thanks for the advice," he retorted. "And if I see the boy on the beach, I'll give him your picture, I promise. You never know."

He ran down the stairs as the girls giggled loudly behind his back. His grandmother awaited him at the bottom, holding a closed paper bag.

"Sammy, what have you been up to? You're going to miss your tournament! You aren't sick, are you?"

"Everything's fine, Grandma. I just overslept. Dad hasn't called, has he?"

For a fraction of a second, his grandmother dropped her eyes. "No, darling, he hasn't. Maybe at noon."

"Will you tell him to pick me up at the gym?"

"Yes, of course." But there was as much enthusiasm in her voice as if he'd asked her to have Superman fly in for lunch. "Here, Sammy, I made your sandwiches. Run along now, or you'll never get there on time. And above all, be careful — not like last year."

Sam bit his tongue to keep from answering. He kissed his grandmother, grabbed his skateboard, and went out.

He caught his bus at the very last moment, just before it pulled away from the curb. Once wedged on the bench at the back, Sam stared out at the landscape of identical little houses passing by the window. Ten days earlier, Allan Faulkner had suddenly left on one of his business trips, and since then he hadn't communicated with anyone — not an e-mail, not a phone call, not even a postcard. It wasn't the first time this had happened, but still, ten days!

The family liked to say that Allan was the original eccentric. That when he was five, he would follow a dog in the street for miles before noticing that he was lost. That when he was ten, he started a revolting collection of fingernail clippings, and boldly wrote to an unbelievable number of celebrities, asking them to send him samples. Worse, some of them had responded: a tennis player, a female rock singer, a television news anchor. He archived the precious relics in a red binder that Grandma still kept in the attic — each scrap in a little transparent packet with the name, date, and cover letter. Allan had even watched the evening news for several days in a row, trying to guess which of the anchor's fingers had supplied the tiny piece of nail. Personally, Sam was inclined to think it had been donated by some anonymous mailroom assistant.

The problem was, his father wasn't ten years old anymore. He was big enough to have quit collecting nail clippings or chasing after dogs, and to say where he was if he had to go away for a few days. But ever since the death of Sam's mother, Allan seemed almost to be living in another world. At first Grandma claimed it was grief, and that he would get over it in time; yet three years after the car crash, they had to admit it was getting worse. He, who used to be so cheerful, always up for a bicycle race or a game of Burnout on the PlayStation, had closed up as tight as an oyster. Sam's grandparents were well aware of this, and at the beginning of the year had persuaded Allan to let Sam come live with them. He had halfheartedly resisted, but eventually agreed; he really was in no condition to take care of his son. He barely managed to open his book-store two or three times a week, and then only when Grandma urged him to, or one of his regular customers harassed him on the telephone. Sadness, said Grandma; lack of character, retorted Aunt Evelyn, Lily's mother; deep depression, judged the doctor.

And ten days earlier, Allan had vanished. These sudden disappearances weren't unusual for him, but they rarely lasted more than two or three days. He usually came back loaded with presents, explaining that he had had to make a super-urgent trip down to the United States to get such-and-such rare book that someone had ordered. Grandma listened to him indulgently and gave him two big kisses, and Sam was too happy to have him home to say anything about it.

Except that this time, Allan didn't seem to be com-ing back — and what's more, it was Sam's birthday. Could a father forget his own son's birthday, even if he *was* the original eccentric?

Sam got off the bus in front of the skating rink. If he hur-ried, he'd arrive at the gymnasium just in time. He rolled his skateboard onto the pavement and slalomed at top speed through passersby, shopping carts, stray children, and grocery bags. He scraped a couple of curbs, leaped a cement bench, and prepared to take the turn that led to the gymnasium. A piece of cake; he'd done it a hundred times before. The town square fence on the right, a little slope to get momentum, the cross street right after that, and . . .

Bang! A violent collision, a screech of metal, and Sam wound up on his stomach, feeling as if the entire square had just landed on his head. He must have run into an old scooter or a garbage can or . . .

"What the . . ."

Cautiously, Sam got to his feet. *A talking garbage can?*

"Oh, man! It's that punk, Faulkner!"

"Don't do it, Monk!" a girl's voice cried.

Monk! He had managed to run into Monk! Driven by a survival instinct he didn't know he had, Sam leaped aside just as Monk lunged at him, the young woman tugging on Monk's shoulders.

"No, Monk! No!"

"I'm going to pound him into the pavement!"

"What's this, what's this?" barked a tall, bearded man in a dark suit.

"He did it on purpose!" yelled Monk. "He ran into me on purpose! Look what he did!" He pointed to his backpack, which had spilled some metal parts and what looked like computer circuits onto the sidewalk. "You saw what happened, sir! Those cost me a fortune!"

As Monk ranted, the girl who had tried to restrain him approached Sam. "Are you okay? No harm done?"

Sam recognized her from the Sainte-Mary judo club. Her name was Cathy, and she sometimes helped teach the youngest classes. She was quite pretty and smiled all the time, and Sam had trouble imagining her spending time with Monk.

"I . . . no, everything's fine, thanks," he babbled. "I was late for the tournament and . . ."

"The tournament? Didn't anyone tell you it was postponed?"

"Postponed? The tournament was postponed?"

"I thought they let everybody know! The Fontana team wasn't able to come; their van broke down two days ago. The competition's happening next Saturday. Didn't you get a message on your answering machine?"

6

"Er, no. Well, maybe my father . . ."

But Sam stopped himself. The club must have phoned the bookstore, because that's the address he'd given when he signed up. And he didn't feel like explaining to Cathy or anyone else that his father wasn't around.

". . . must have forgotten," he muttered between clenched teeth.

Cathy bent down to retrieve his skateboard, which was jammed into the square's fence like a sword.

"It looks okay, that's something. You could have really messed each other up."

"LET ME GO!" screamed Monk, who didn't seem to have calmed down at all. "That little jerk is going to pay for my gear, and then —"

"You'd better get out of here," whispered Cathy, slipping the skateboard under Sam's arm. "It's going to take a while before he cools down."

"But what about you? Won't he . . . ?"

"Don't worry, I know how to handle him. And nothing says the circuit boards are actually screwed up. We were going to upgrade the club's computers. Monk's a computer genius, you know."

Monk, good at computers? So he actually had a brain?

The girl was still smiling.

"As soon as he gets working, he'll forget all about you. Go on, get out of here. We'll see you on Saturday."

She gave a little wave, and Sam left as quickly as he could. But he could hear Monk's explosion behind him: "SAM FAULKNER, YOU LOSER! YOU'LL PAY FOR THIS WITH YOUR TEETH!"

CHAPTER TWO

The Stone Statue

Allan Faulkner's bookstore was located on Barenboim Street, in an old Sainte-Mary neighborhood that had been going downhill for the last thirty or forty years. It was an odd choice of location for a bookstore — a tiny two-story Victorian house with dingy blue columns and faded shutters, wedged between two even more run-down houses. Every other business worthy of the name had long ago deserted the street; the only residents now were little old people, as shabby as the fronts of their houses. They set out like ghosts early in the morning, then returned around nine o'clock with their shopping bags of groceries, hurrying home to lock themselves in.

Given the setting, the bookstore's opening hadn't exactly generated much neighborhood enthusiasm — a hello or a good evening at most, plus a few sour comments when a customer parked partly on the sidewalk or when Sam scraped his skateboard along the curbs on his way home from school. Only Max, an old, nearly deaf man who lived three houses up, bothered making conversation with the Faulkners.

As Sam skateboarded down the street, he wondered yet

again why his father had chosen this neglected part of town. To protect himself, suggested Grandma, and to keep away from the noise of the world. Within a month of his wife's death, Allan had sold their pretty house in the Bel View suburb of Sainte-Mary — too many memories of Elisa — and gone looking for a place to set up his bookstore. This was a refuge for him, really. But it was an oppressive refuge when you're thirteen years old — well, fourteen now — you've just lost your mother, and what gets you going are the things happening downtown: bright lights and nonstop activity.

Sam stopped outside the bookstore, climbed the stoop, and surveyed his surroundings. Nothing was stirring. He wasn't sure that coming here was a very good idea. Shouldn't he have alerted his grandmother first? But the tournament was canceled, he had the whole day in front of him, and it was his birthday. What was wrong with dropping by his place? Because it *was* his place, wasn't it? Pick up a few CDs, check on his things . . . *And make sure Dad hadn't come home unexpectedly,* added a little inner voice. *Or left any clues about his departure.* Grandpa had stopped by the bookstore twice this week, but it was always possible. . . .

Sam turned the key in the lock. The door squeaked on its hinges, and the FAULKNER'S ANTIQUE BOOKS sign swayed above the frame.

"Dad?"

Everything was quiet. He crossed the entryway, then the large room with its bookshelves lined up exactly as in a library. There were tables and chairs where you could sit and look at books, and two sofas with halogen lights for reading comfortably. A good portion of the money from the Bel View house was here, in these yellowed old papers and leather bindings. How his father managed to accumulate so many of them was a mystery, as was his ability to attract the occasional customer. More than likely, Sam's grandparents kicked some money in from time to time.

Sam went into the kitchen. Everything was in order. The dishwasher was empty, and from the sucking sound the seal made when he opened it, it probably hadn't been used in several days. The refrigerator was practically bare, except for some expired containers of yogurt, a package of sausages in plastic — *sealed in plastic*, Grandma corrected him in his mind — and two cans of beer. No recent feast there. Sam went upstairs, and couldn't avoid feeling a pang upon entering his bedroom. There were his Tony Hawk and *Lord of the Rings* posters on the wall; his collection of miniature antique cars — very different from fingernail clippings; his drawings; and his guitar from the days when he had clumsily tried to learn to play. But he wasn't here to mope about his past. He stuck two old CDs in his bag, just to say he'd done so, and went to inspect his father's office. Unfortunately, there was no letter of explanation on the desk pad, no papers about his departure in the drawers, no Internet itinerary in the trash can. The three big yellow suitcases hadn't been moved. He found one odd thing on the floor of his father's closet: a pile of white linen tunics and drawstring pants, clothes that Sam had never seen his father wear. But the rest of his wardrobe hung limply on its hangers.

Stranger and stranger . . . Had his father left for a trip without a change of clothes? Or had he planned to be away only a few hours, or a day at most? Because his toothbrush was there, too, completely dry, as well as the toothpaste and electric razor. Unless . . . Sam momentarily had a terrible vision of a car crumpled at the bottom of a ravine, but he pushed the image away. No, nothing serious could have happened to his father. Wasn't he the original eccentric? And eccentrics always pull through, Grandpa had said. There had to be some other explanation.

Sam went downstairs again and stopped by the hall table where the telephone lay. The silver answering machine was blinking: 20 MESSAGES — MEMORY FULL.

Sam pushed the PLAY button. There was some background static, then a click: "Mr. Faulkner? I stopped by your bookstore last week and I saw a copy of *Twenty Thousand Leagues Under the Sea* that I wanted . . ."

Beep! Sam skipped to the next message: "Is this Antique Books on Barenboim Street? I'd like to know your hours, because I'm looking for a rare edition of . . ."

Beep! Next message. "Allan? This is Thomas Mourre. Were you able to find the Plantin Bible I ordered from you? Because I have to . . ."

Beep! And so on. Most of the messages were from customers or people looking for things, plus one wrong number, an advertising pitch — "Er, Mr. Faulkner? If you ever plan to replace your windows or shutters, our company will take . . ." — a request for a meeting from a banker who clearly wasn't in a good mood, and three attempts by Grandma to reach her son. All the messages were more than eight days old. The one from the judo club wasn't there, for a very good reason: There was no room left on the tape.

One call stood out from the rest. A far-off metallic voice,

distorted by distance or bad line quality: "Allan? It's me. . . . I know that you're there. . . . Stop being a jerk, Allan, answer me. Allan, can you hear me? Allan? Pick up, for God's sake!" A long pause, then: "All right, I've warned you. . . ."

The mysterious caller then hung up. Sam replayed the tape several times. The call had been made the day after his father's disappearance. The tone was threatening and, what was more upsetting, almost familiar. But Sam couldn't imagine who the voice could belong to. Was there some connection with his father's departure? Maybe, given the warning; maybe not, considering that Allan couldn't have heard any of these messages. So then what?

Sam had an idea. His father hadn't owned a car for the last three years, and he often took taxis to the train station or the airport. Taxi companies were required to keep a record of their trips — Sam had read that in a detective story — so if the last call his father made was to a taxi company, it might be possible to learn where he'd gone. . . . He pushed the phone's REDIAL button to repeat the last outgoing number.

"Hello?" bawled a hoarse voice at the other end of the line.

If that was the company's switchboard operator, she had better quit smoking — like right away.

"Yes, hello," Sam began. "I'm calling for some information —"

"What?" shouted the voice, sounding bewildered.

"I'd like some information, please. My father telephoned you a few days ago and —"

"Jumping Jehoshaphat, speak up!"

Jumping Jehoshaphat . . . It was Max! The neighbor who was deaf as a post!

"Max? Max, is that you?"

"What's this about?"

"Max, it's Sam, Allan Faulkner's son, from Antique Books. My father must have called you about ten days ago —"

"Teak hooks? I don't need anything, as it happens, and certainly no hooks! Darn salesman!"

And the line went dead.

Sam held the phone for a few seconds. His father must have called Max to give him a set of keys and ask him to water the flowers or something like that. But what if he had also told Max where he was going? Even if the old man was hard to follow, Sam didn't have any other clues.

Sam grabbed his bag and was about to go when he saw the door to the basement, the one place he hadn't checked. He hesitated for a moment, then dropped his bag, switched on the light, and descended the two flights of stairs to the storage area. Allan used it to hold piles of volumes on steel racks, plus a supply of empty cartons and materials for repairing books, and had hung a heavy tapestry on the back wall, probably to keep the damp and cold out. Sam had been down to the cellar only a couple of times, and then mostly when they had first moved in; it was entirely his father's domain. Anyway, there was nobody there today.

He began to climb back up the stairs, but changed his mind halfway. There was something wrong. The storage area didn't look the way it usually did, or at least not the way he remembered it. . . . It appeared to have gotten smaller. That seemed ridiculous, but the only subject Sam really excelled at in school was drawing, and he had a good eye for spaces. He walked to the back wall, counting his steps: *one, two, three, four, five* . . . It didn't add up; the basement ought to be at least seven yards deep. Which meant that . . .

He walked over to the tapestry, a reproduction of a medieval hanging with a unicorn and a beautiful princess. He poked it with his finger and felt something hard. No, the wall was there, all right; he must be imagining things. He knocked, but the sound was distinctly hollow. Had his father added a partition and hidden it behind the curtain? But to hide what? Another storage area? For even more valuable books?

Sam lifted the heavy curtain and slipped underneath. It was a partition all right, made of do-it-yourself drywall panels. He ran his hands over its surface, gradually moving to the right. After two yards, he felt hinges: a door. Heart pounding, he pushed it open.

"Dad?"

The new room was empty. It was lit by a little lamp and very minimally furnished: a cot, a stool, and that was it. Sam was relieved not to find his father unconscious or worse, but a thousand questions crowded his mind. He walked over to the cot and noticed a big book lying on the floor. Sam picked it up, brought it closer to the light — no title, no author, just a thick, cracked red cover — and opened it at random. It seemed to be a book of history: CRIMES AND PUNISHMENT DURING THE REIGN OF VLAD TEPES. He quickly scanned the double page, which showed various tortures practiced by a certain Vlad Tepes in the fifteenth century, somewhere in Wallachia, wherever that was. It was an old volume, but not that old; maybe a hundred years, to judge by the typeface and printing. His father was a history buff, but would he really lock himself in this miserable storage room to read the exploits of some bloodthirsty Wallachian?

Sam picked up a flashlight hanging on a hook and slowly played it over the rest of the room. There was nothing else except a grayish shape sunk into the earth in the far corner: a big stone, about twenty inches high, shaped like a keyhole and rounded at the top. He went over to examine it. It looked like a totem or a voodoo object, the kind of thing you see in horror films, where a terrible curse will strike whomever discovers it. Only its front was decorated. On the top half, a carved sun shot out a half-dozen slits that looked like rays. At the bottom, a cavity about two hands deep had been hollowed out of the stone. The whole thing might have passed for a Paleolithic peanut dispenser, but without the peanuts. It didn't make any sense, unless his father had suddenly joined a cult.

As Sam shone his flashlight around the stone, a shiny round piece of metal a few inches away caught his eye. He picked it up and turned it over in his palm. It was a dirty coin, with a hole in the middle and a pattern of entwined lines and symbols that suggested Arabic writing, but exactly what country it could have come from was a mystery. . . . In any case, it seemed neither very ancient nor very valuable. Maybe the strange stone was a traditional game from some far-off country: You threw a coin and it was supposed to land either in the main cavity — that counted less — or in one of the rays — that counted more. Really exciting.

Sam tried to slip the coin into a slit, but it fell out. He tried again on the other rays and got the same result. The only other place it could go . . . Somewhat dubiously, he put the coin in the center of the sun. It fit perfectly, as if held there by an invisible force.

Good, he said to himself. *We're making progress.*

It was then that he heard a kind of humming coming from — the stone? He leaned closer, and yes, it seemed to be producing a very regular, distant vibration. Moreover, it felt as if it were giving off something — heat — and a kind of magnetism. . . . He even had the feeling that the ground around him was starting to vibrate and that all he had to do was put his fingers on the stone. He stretched out his hand . . .

A terrible fire ran up Sam's arm and set his body ablaze.

CHAPTER THREE

Iona

Sam fell to his knees, his guts in knots and his body racked with spasms. His arm still burned as he vomited painfully, uncontrollably, onto the thick green grass under his hands.

Wait a minute. . . . *Grass?*

When Sam was finally able to raise his head, he nearly fainted. He wasn't in the storage room anymore. He wasn't anywhere he knew. A rocky beach with a thin strip of sand and a vast sea stretched away in the distance, and he seemed to be halfway up a wild outcropping of rocks and thick grass. What had happened to him? And what had happened to his *clothes*? Instead of his jeans and T-shirt, he was now wearing a sweat-soaked long shirt that covered his arms and legs, and itched as well. And what about his burns? He could still feel the sting of the fire that had consumed him when he'd touched the stone, and yet his skin was miraculously whole, as smooth as a baby's. As if it all had been nothing but a dream.

Shakily he stood up. The strange stone statue stood a couple of yards away. Except that it didn't look quite the same anymore. It was a little taller, a little blacker, but it bore the same markings: a sun with raylike slits and a dark cavity at the bottom. Sam felt a surge of hope: This was a dream, of course, but if he put the coin back in the center of the sun, it would end and everything would return to normal. He carefully searched the grass around him, but there was no sign of the coin. He looked further, picked up pebbles, dug under rocks with his hands. Nothing. He tried stones of various shapes, but none matched the sun's diameter. He swore, cursed the stone, and finally burst into tears. This was no dream . . . this was no dream!

It took Sam several long minutes to calm down. Whatever had actually happened to him, he figured, crying wouldn't help him deal with it. After all, he was alive, wasn't he? And he was starting to feel cold.

He stood up, brushed himself off, and began climbing the slope, the better to see around him. At the top, he found that he was on a fairly large island, treeless, windswept, green and gray. Beyond it, the infinite rolling of waves; above, a sky heavy with clouds, pierced here and there by shafts of golden light. And in the distance, at the other end of the island — houses! There was smoke—there were even people! He could see them!

"HEY!" he screamed. "Hello! Hey!"

But the distance was too great and the wind was against him. Sam started to run, unconcerned about his bare feet, which sank into the soft earth of the moor. The island was inhabited! It would all be explained to him! Perhaps he had suffered some sort of attack in the basement, and been taken out of Sainte-Mary by helicopter, and the paramedics had given him the shirt. . . . An accident had happened, and . . . he had survived, that was the important thing, and these people were going to take care of him. He could dry himself off and phone Grandma to reassure her. She must be beside herself with worry!

After ten minutes of running, Sam forced himself to slow down. The village was now just a few hundred yards away. It wasn't really a village either, more like a collection of huts surrounded by a rough log wall, with a stone building with a bell tower in the middle. Was it a camping resort? A community of back-to-the-land hippies?

He stopped completely. He saw a group of people gathered near what looked like a sheep pen just outside the stockade. They were pointing at him and talking. They were all men, and dressed in long brown robes with odd-looking rope belts. Sam slapped his forehead. They were monks, of course! An island with monks! Wait until his father heard about this!

He continued on his way, but cautiously. He couldn't remember any monasteries in the area around Sainte-Mary. His attack must have been very serious for him to be sent so far from home! Maybe he'd been unconscious for several days. Yet in spite of the vomiting, he didn't feel so bad.

The group of men were walking toward him now. Some brandished staffs or swords. Sam's stomach tightened again. He had once seen a program about Middle Ages fanatics who got together on weekends to live the way they did during the Crusades. It had sort of sounded like fun, even though some of the people seemed a little wacko. But here he didn't have any choice; there was nobody else on the island. Their voices reached him now, scraps of sentences carried by the whirling gusts of wind:

"Dia duit . . ."

"Dia is Muire duit . . ."

It sounded almost like the Elvish spoken in *The Lord of the Rings.*

"Beannacht Colm Cille! Acht bhí . . ."

Sam cleared his throat and timidly raised his hand in greeting. "Hey there!" They were now only about twenty yards away.

". . . uaignigh na h-Alban?"

It was then that something happened that was odder than everything else. Without making the slightest effort, *Sam began to understand what the men were saying!* One moment, it was an unknown guttural language, and the next it was as if he'd been speaking it from birth!

"I told you so!" exclaimed a somewhat hunchbacked man with a beard. "He just appeared like that, all at once, in Colm Cille's cove!"

"He's one of their spies," another burst out, glaring accusingly at Sam. "He came as a scout. He came to rob us!"

"That's enough!" interrupted the one in front. "Let's hear what he has to tell us. Maybe God, in his infinite mercy, is sending us his last messenger. Where are you from, boy?"

"He must have been shipwrecked here," a tall, thin man broke in before Sam had time to speak. "In this season, fishing boats crisscross the sea and . . ."

"Will you be quiet, Ranald Tallman?" cut in the leader. "He looks clever enough to explain himself."

Sam struggled to control the shaking he felt rising up his legs. When he spoke, what language would come out of his mouth? And how *could* he explain his presence on the island?

"I . . . I did wash up here," he said in a whisper — a whisper that sounded distinctly Elvish. "My . . . my boat capsized."

"You see!" said Ranald Tallman approvingly.

"That's a lie!" the hunchback shouted. "He appeared all at once!"

"Come now, Brother Egrin, you must admit that you no longer have the eyes of your youth!" the leader objected. "And if it is Colm Cille's cove, that may be a sign. Our venerable master has always watched over us, hasn't he, brothers?"

"Yes, Father Abbot," agreed the others all together.

"Despite the perilous times we are living in, nothing evil could come from the cove of Colm Cille. The Lord would never allow our enemies to profane such a sacred place. So unless proven otherwise, we shall assume this boy was indeed shipwrecked on our island. And who knows what his arrival may be worth to us? The ways of God are full of twists and turns, but they always follow the paths of wisdom."

Turning to Sam, he said, "What is your name, my boy?"

He hesitated. "Sam."

"*Saum,*" repeated the abbot with a sonorous *aum*. "And have you been baptized, Saum?"

"Yes," said Sam, nodding. He pronounced the word "yes" as "*Tá,*" but was barely aware of having done so.

"So you know the sign of the cross?"

They were all looking at him curiously and Sam thought it best to demonstrate. He moved three fingers from his forehead to his chest and then to each shoulder. Murmurs punctuated with "Amen!" greeted his gesture, and the swords and staffs lowered as if by enchantment.

The abbot smiled at him.

"That's perfect, Saum. I see you are a good Christian, and not one of those savages of Satan. So you were on a fishing boat, is that right?"

Sam agreed. What else could he say?

"Well, Saum, you will now be part of the community here on Iona — but with some restrictions. You will sleep in the stable, where Brother Artair will give you a proper robe and a measure of hay. You are formally forbidden from entering the dormitory and the storeroom, and you may enter the church or the scriptorium only when accompanied by one of us — Brother Ranald, for example. Indeed, since he showed himself so eager to defend you, he will now be responsible for you . . . with the duties and restrictions that implies, of course."

There was a kind of warning in these words, which Brother Ranald appeared to understand, because he bowed deferentially.

"Unfortunately for you, Saum," continued the abbot, "our island welcomes you at its darkest hour. The White Strangers are on their way here even now. They have sacked other monasteries and towns two days' sailing from here. But we are by far the richest community, as they well know. I fear you may regret linking your destiny with ours, Saum."

He smiled sadly and gave Sam a pat on the back that felt paternal, but which nearly knocked him over. "God is testing us, my boy! We may have to fight. But tonight the horizon is clear, and we can sleep peacefully."

He turned away to take the path back to the village, but Sam was burning to know more. "Excuse me, Father Abbot. Could you please . . ."

The abbot spun around, his brows knitted in a fierce

frown. "The first rule you must learn, Saum the Fisherman, is silence," he thundered. "No one here speaks unless I ask him a question, or if he must in order to do his work. And especially not within the abbey boundaries. Will you remember that? Brother Ranald, see to it that your charge respects the law henceforth."

Ranald hurried over to Sam and with a glance enjoined him to humbly lower his eyes.

Sam had to face facts: This wasn't just a weekend with some costumed weirdos. These people were real monks. But backward monks, who must have come from Planet Cow Pie to be willing to live under these conditions! Their community was really just a collection of plank cabins in the middle of a mountain of mud. Only the stone church in the center, with its odd bell tower, vaguely suggested civilization. As for the rest of it . . .

Brother Artair led Sam to the stable, where he prepared Sam's bed by tossing an armload of hay at the feet of the solitary cow. He also gave him a thick wool blanket, a moth-eaten robe with a hood, a long linen tunic, short linen pants, and some prehistoric flip-flops, and ordered him to stay in the stable until the evening meal. From the disgusted way he treated him, Sam guessed that Artair, like Egrin the hunchback, hadn't swallowed the sudden appearance of the boy-from-nowhere. And they weren't wrong, in a way. . . .

The stable's only window was barred by a shutter, but Sam was able to peek through the cracks in the wood to see the monks' comings and goings in the gathering darkness. He counted some fifteen or twenty brothers of various ages, most of them fairly short except for the abbot and Brother Ranald.

Each seemed to know his role by heart and had no need to speak. Some carried tubs or heavy sacks; others reinforced the stockade by planting new stakes; still others went in and out of the church, and some worked in a large building located at the foot of the bell tower. All this took place in total silence, except for the *splugh!* of their sandals squelching through the mud.

Sam no longer knew what to think. He had heard of an Iona somewhere in Nova Scotia, but that was over seven hundred miles from Sainte-Mary. And whatever had brought him to the island, it didn't explain the mystery of this crazy abbey or the abbot's words. Who were these White Strangers? What were the dangers the monks seemed to dread? *And above all, how was Sam able to understand their bizarre language?*

The stable door suddenly burst open. "Saum?" whispered Ranald Tallman. "It's suppertime, hurry up. And not a word!"

Sam rose and followed him through the gloom to a long building next to the kitchens: the dining hall. When he entered, all the men turned toward him. There were more of them than he had thought, about thirty at least, spread between two long tables. The abbot sat in the back, alone, and another monk stood at the front before an enormous book on a reading desk. Egrin the hunchback, who was seated nearest the door on the right, shot Sam a poisonous look. Brother Ranald led him toward the left-hand bench. As soon as they were seated, the duty monk began his reading. Sam supposed that it must be a Latin text, but unlike "Iona Elvish," he couldn't grasp a single word of it. The simultaneous translator that had sprouted in his head apparently couldn't be set for two languages at the same time.

The cook monk then appeared, carrying a heavy pot. He

made the rounds, filling bowls one after the other with a savory soup full of dark herbs that looked almost like hair. Sam never ate soup at home. But he was starving, and he could feel thirty pairs of eyes on him, so he bravely stuck his spoonlike utensil into the steaming liquid, drew out a good hunk of twisted greens, and swallowed it whole.

That turned out to be a mistake. It scalded his palate — a second-degree burn, at least — and the taste was incredibly bitter, like a concentration of the worst cabbages he'd ever eaten. And of course there was no way to spit it out. Sam gritted his teeth, felt the tears rising to his eyes, and managed to get it all down by holding his nose — with third-degree burns to his throat! He tried to wash it down with the contents of the heavy mug in front of him, but *that* contained some kind of revolting liquor that tasted like manure and made him gag. Ranald Tallman gave him a discreet kick under the table, and Sam resolved not to touch any more soup.

After that, he nibbled only on a tiny scrap of meat he managed to rescue from a horrible slab of fat, and a piece of cheese that was as hard as stone. "Dessert" was a thick, warm, slightly sugary pudding. It looked inviting, but it landed in his stomach like a block of cement, forcing him to gulp down the contents of his mug. And to think that he complained to Grandma when there wasn't enough ketchup for his French fries!

Once the ordeal of supper was over, Brother Ranald led him back to the stable by the flickering light of a candle. The night was black and starry, and the capricious wind gusted around them, tugging at their robes.

"I'm very sorry, Saum, but I can't leave you the light,"

Ranald murmured. "The abbot won't allow it." He opened the door and stood aside to let Sam enter.

"Still, I brought you this." From under his robe he brought out a quarter loaf of dark bread and put it in Sam's hands. "And there's a bucket above the manger, if you know how to milk a cow."

Ranald said nothing further and quickly latched the door behind him. Sam heard the enormous key squeak in the lock. Now he was alone again — or almost. The cow greeted him with an ear-shattering moo.

As he stumbled toward her in the darkness, Sam realized she was lying on the hay of his bed. It was going to be a very long night.

An hour later, Sam and the cow had each finally secured their share of the hay, and the cow was snoring noisily in the corner. Curled against the opposite wall, Sam tried to sleep himself, but his mind swirled endlessly with thoughts of home. Grandma must know he was gone by now. Would she have called the police? Maybe his disappearance would be on the news, and Alicia would see it and worry about him . . . but thinking of Alicia hurt too much, and he pushed the idea away. Maybe his father had shown up at last and he would be in charge of the search for Sam. And if he hadn't, again: Where could he be?

The cow snorted, and Sam remembered the time his family had gone to a living farm museum near Sainte-Mary. His mother had worn a ridiculous floppy sun hat with large plastic flowers, and as she knelt to pet a baby calf, a cow reached over and gnawed the flowers right off her hat before spitting them out in disgust. Mom had laughed and laughed, and Dad had tipped the hat back to kiss her. . . . Sam smiled, remembering. If Mom were with him in the stable now, she would probably laugh about this too.

As the bell in the tower tolled out, Sam finally fell asleep.

CHAPTER FOUR

Colm Cille's Treasure

Sam would have liked to wake up in his room, under the covers, with the radio blaring: "It's seven o'clock, guys. Time to start moving! And to help you get shaking, coming right up, the latest from Hot Pickles. . . ." Instead, he got a violent slap from a tail and a deafening *moo*. Never mind the noise from the abbey lunatics, who had spent the night walking around the church singing at the top of their lungs — they were only silent during the day! — and ringing bells at all hours. In short, it wasn't a promising start to the day.

He spent the morning locked up with his noisy, smelly girlfriend, with nothing to do besides follow the ballet of the monks from his window. The activity of the day was sword training, and it was like a cross between *Star Wars* (for the costumes) and *Funniest Home Videos* (for results). Once Sam even wondered whether he was watching the filming of a reality television show: "Thirty men, alone on a desert island, have agreed to live like monks in the year 1000! Watch them eat grass, fight in the mud, and sing after midnight! Every Saturday, *you* vote for the new abbot!" And so on.

Except that there wasn't any camera. Or film crew. Or much of anything else.

Toward noon — Sam's stomach was screaming with hunger — Tallman finally showed up, holding a fishing line and hooks.

"Saum," he whispered. "We're going fishing!"

"Fishing . . ."

"Quickly!"

In silence Sam fell into step behind him. If the monks were counting on him to bring back fish, they were going to be disappointed. They left by the rear of the enclosure to avoid the rest of the monks, who were still practicing swordplay. Once away from the abbey, Ranald took a piece of bread and a ration of cheese from his sleeve and handed them to Sam.

"Here, eat this. You probably aren't used to having just one meal a day."

Sam bit avidly into the golden bread and less avidly on the piece of cheese, which was as pale and hard as a shard of bone.

"Don't chew it," Tallman advised. "Let it melt on your tongue."

They strode briskly away from the abbey. As they walked along the intensely green meadows and little stone walls, Sam finally dared to ask his question: "Where are we going?"

"You're not a fisherman's son, are you?" said Ranald by way of answer.

"Well, I . . ."

"No point in lying. I could give you this hand line," he added, holding out the fishing line, "and you wouldn't know what to do with it. Your teeth are too white and your hands too soft to be an ordinary fisherman's."

Sam racked his brains to come up with a plausible story, but drew a blank.

"I don't think the abbot believed you either. He may have decided that he didn't want to know. And Brother Egrin's sight isn't that bad, is it, Saum? You did appear in Colm Cille's cove, didn't you? Do you even know who Colm Cille was?" Sam shook his head. "Colm Cille was a saint. He came from Ireland to found our abbey more than two hundred years ago. He chose Iona as a starting place to bring the word of God to Caledonia. At the time the Picts and the Angles were far from being Christians."

Amid this barrage of names, Sam only recognized one: Ireland. And Ireland, as best he could recall, was in the west of Europe, thousands of miles across the Atlantic from Sainte-Mary. *How had he gotten there?*

"He battled warriors and monsters, spoke with angels and with God. He worked more than one miracle too. Today, monks come from very far away to honor his memory and study at his school. I am from Ireland myself," Ranald continued. "I was supposed to spend three years in the abbey, mastering the books, but now I fear . . ." He gazed far out to sea. "They won't be long in coming."

"Who are 'they'?"

"The White Strangers. We don't really know where they live. Very far to the north, in any case. For the last few months they've sailed up and down the coast in their big boats, pillaging and burning every settlement they find. And they have heard talk of Colm Cille's treasure."

"A treasure?"

"A treasure, yes; the most sumptuous and richest in the

country. I will show it to you, if you like. Do you see the cove over there?"

He was pointing to the small bay where Sam had arrived, four or five hundred yards away to the left.

"That's where Colm Cille came to the island. And you see that little hill to the right? That's where we're going to hide the treasure. Follow me, I'll explain."

They began to climb among the huge rocks of a hill that faced the ocean. Behind one of the biggest boulders was a crack the width of a man, leading into a kind of cave with an arched entryway. A long tunnel of rock in the ceiling admitted a narrow shaft of light into the room, whose walls twisted away into the dark. Two thin logs wedged between two boulders supported the arch. A hatchet was propped against the wood.

"The White Strangers offer no mercy," Ranald said quietly. "Those they don't kill, they enslave. It is even said that they sell their captives and their prizes to those who worship Muhammad. But they won't get the Colm Cille treasure."

Sam looked as deeply into the cave as he could, but he saw no sign of treasure.

"And this treasure, where is it?"

"We will bring the most beautiful items here this afternoon. And high time, if you ask me."

"But how can you be sure these White Strangers won't find your hiding place?"

"Because I will stop them," Ranald said, a hint of defiance in his voice. "As soon as their sails appear in the south, I'll run up here and chop the beams in the arch, and the entryway will crash shut. They can search the island from top to bottom, but they will never get their hands on the treasure."

"But what about you?" said Sam. "How will you escape?"

Ranald pointed to the natural chimney that let in the shaft of light. "With the help of the Lord, I will rise into the air. That's also why the abbot chose me: I am the tallest and most limber of the monks."

Tallman, thought Sam.

"And what if you aren't able to get out?"

"In that case I will die, as my brothers will probably die fighting the heathens. But at least Colm Cille's treasure will be spared." He looked at Sam, smiling. "Don't look so upset, boy! Your sudden arrival has given us new hope — at least some of us. As we stand on the eve of confronting our enemies, your appearance on the island can't be chance. Colm Cille must have guided your footsteps."

Brother Ranald's tone was almost respectful, and Sam guessed that in their distress, some of the monks were according him an importance he didn't have. That said, if it earned him a little indulgence, it was all to the good.

When they had left their fish at the kitchen back at the abbey — Tallman was expert at handling a fishing line — he gestured to Sam to follow him to the building at the base of the church.

"Now," he whispered as he opened the door, "come see Colm Cille's treasure!"

It was the abbey's scriptorium. Sam was slack-jawed with astonishment. If only his father were there! He who almost fainted at a mere glimpse of an ancient book . . . he would have died from bliss in the presence of the great illustrated volumes before Sam's eyes. These monks must be the only people still working this way! A multitude of oil lamps hung from chains on the ceiling, casting a soft light over the room. Some of the monks were seated on little stools, leaning forward uncomfortably to recopy existing books on great rolls of yellow parchment. A second group worked with the cut parchments, folding and gathering them into booklets that, once assembled, formed the volumes. A third group of monks stood at tall desks, using confident brushstrokes to decorate the texts. To the sides, rough bookshelves held dozens of finished copies or volumes yet to be reproduced. A few had embossed silver covers.

Egrin the hunchback looked up as Ranald led Sam to a tilted table all the way at the back. It bore a book more beautiful than any Sam had ever seen before. Its embossed solid-gold binding showed a religious figure with two fingers raised, surrounded by angels and fantastic animals. The book was encrusted with dozens of blue, red, and green jewels, some of them the size of your thumb. Colm Cille's treasure!

"This is our most beautiful copy of the Gospels," whispered Tallman.

"Brother Ranald," growled Egrin. "The rule!"

Ranald paid no attention to Egrin's remark, and the hunchback left the scriptorium, grumbling under his breath. Under Sam's dazzled eyes, Tallman unsnapped the heavy clasps and opened the book. The pages were gorgeous, their beautiful antique writing decorated with a profusion of delicate images. Sam didn't know much about his father's business, but even if this was just a copy, a book like this must be worth a fortune!

He had been looking at the book for only a few minutes when the door slammed behind them. The abbot entered, flanked by the hunchback.

"Brother Ranald," began the abbot. "Regardless of the

circumstances, this boy must not trouble the peace of our scriptorium. Take him back to the stable and lock him in until the evening meal."

"But, Father Abbot, you yourself said that . . ."

"Be content to obey, Ranald, or you will both be doing penance. The afternoon is wearing on, and it is time to carry our volumes to safety. Have the bell rung and tell everyone to gather in the scriptorium. As for you, my boy," he said to Sam, "you heard me. I don't want to see you again before the evening meal."

Just behind the abbot, Egrin the hunchback rubbed his hands, a triumphant glint in his eyes.

Sam left the stable only for dinner that night. The next morning, he awoke with a start, his face drenched with sweat. His stomach was making awful noises; the revolting cabbage broth wasn't sitting very well. . . . He cast a glance sideways at the shutter: It was barely dawn.

Then he realized that the groans weren't coming from his belly.

He jumped to his feet and rushed to the window. He could hear shouts and yells and the heavy clash of weapons. Gripped with panic, he had to concentrate to force the shutter open. The White Strangers had landed! Though there was only a handful of them, they were tall and strong, and wore helmets with visors that protected their heads. The unarmored monks were defending themselves as best they could, with some barricading themselves in the church and others engaged in desperate hand-to-hand combat.

The stable door flew open and the cow mooed with terror.

"Saum! Saum!" It was Tallman, holding a sword. He locked the door behind him and ran over, panting. "They surprised us at dawn. We weren't ready! Someone lit a fire to guide them! The abbey has been overrun!"

Boom! A violent blow shook the door.

"You have to save the treasure, Saum, or these barbarians will take it!"

"Me? But *you* were supposed to go to the cave!" Sam sputtered. "I could never . . ."

Boom! A second blow to the door. Tallman pulled his robe up his leg, revealing a bloody ankle. "I can't, I won't be fast enough. You're quick, you'll have a chance to slip away."

Boom! The wooden planks were beginning to crack, and the cow started mooing again.

"And you'll be safer at the cave," added Ranald, taking him by the arm. "Now stand against the wall, and as soon as the door gives way . . ."

The doorframe shattered and a shouting, armor-clad figure burst into the room.

"Go, Saum!" ordered Brother Ranald as he struck the intruder with his sword.

Legs flailing, Sam launched himself into the gloom. Metal clanged all around him. He hid behind a barrel, then ran, crouching, along the stockade. Once he reached the back of the enclosure, he lifted the gate that led to the fields and began to run at top speed.

When he reached the first stone wall, he threw himself to the ground to catch his breath. It wasn't very light yet; surely no one could see him. But when he turned around, he spotted a monk at the stockade entrance. The monk wasn't fighting;

on the contrary, he seemed to be talking with a group of the White Strangers. It was Egrin — Egrin the hunchback, who had betrayed his brothers! Egrin, who must have lit the fire that guided the pillagers. Egrin, who was now pointing in Sam's direction . . .

Head down, Sam resumed his flight. With a little luck, the White Strangers wouldn't have spotted him. Who could these invaders be, for that matter? What century was Iona living in?

As he rounded the rocky spur that blocked his view, Sam suddenly had his answer. To the west, two long boats with sculpted prows were pulled up on shore, their slender lines and rectangular, bloodred sails leaving no doubt: dragon ships! Dragon ships, like in the history books! The White Strangers were *VIKINGS*!

Sam fell, sprawling on the cool grass. Everything he had refused to accept until then was suddenly, undeniably clear. The abbey, the scriptorium, the monks, the Vikings . . . he had gone back in time! *He had gone back in time!*

He shot a quick glance behind him. While the other warriors had entered the stockade, one had set off after him, carrying a three-foot sword and a shield. Where Egrin had been standing, a vaguely human shape lay curled on the ground. The invaders had settled accounts with their accomplice.

Sam started running again. An orangey sun was now licking the gray ocean, giving the coast an unreal glow. The shore he was supposed to reach seemed to be at the other end of the world. Without slowing down, he glanced back at the warrior behind him; Sam had a comfortable lead, but his legs were half the length of his pursuer's. He pounded up the trail he had taken with Tallman the day before. How far away that fishing trip seemed now!

Finally, he caught sight of the hill above the sea. The Viking was still a good four or five hundred yards behind him. Either he was confident of catching his prey, or he wasn't good at footraces.

Panting, Sam climbed up the rocks. Where the heck was the entrance to the cave? There, a little higher. He slipped into the crack in the rocks and almost stumbled over the new additions to the room: about ten low tables bearing the monastery's books. Quick, the hatchet! He grabbed its handle and took a clumsy swing at the first and thinnest of the beams over the entryway. What if it didn't work? What if the logs wouldn't give way? He redoubled his effort, and a decent-size notch appeared in the wood. Again, and again! The first beam yielded with a crack. The mass of rocks above the entrance trembled, but that was all. Sam rubbed his hands: He had huge blisters on his palms. The White Stranger must be very close now. He attacked the second beam, which vibrated violently under each of his blows. What if the entire wall crashed down on him without warning? But just as he thought this, the arch abruptly collapsed with a roar, and Sam barely had time to jump backward. A ton of rocks now sealed the entryway. He had won!

When the cloud of dust had settled a little and he had caught his breath, Sam checked to see that he hadn't caused too much damage. Only one of the tables was broken, a few books knocked to the ground. Automatically he stacked them up — the reflex of a bookseller's son. The smallest of these books had an unusual format: It was very long, with a ring through one end of the spine — to hang it from your belt, perhaps? Inside, curiously enough, the same page was repeated twenty times: a drawing of an island that might be Iona, with a commentary. Too bad Sam wasn't able to read Latin. Suddenly he froze. There was a noise outside, a muffled pounding. The Viking must have heard the crash. . . . Was he already starting to clear away the rocks?

Sam looked around for something to defend himself with. He had the hatchet, of course, and that piece of beam might serve as a club if necessary. Otherwise there was nothing but books, some of them wrapped in leather — the most precious volumes, Sam supposed. Inspecting the place more carefully, he eventually discovered a chest hidden in a recess in the wall. He carried it under the shaft of light and opened it. Coins — gold and silver coins. It was the monastery's other treasure! As Sam stirred them with his finger, he noticed a coin that had a hole in the middle, which seemed about the same diameter as . . . Yes! The same as the one he had used the other day in his father's basement! The coin that fit perfectly onto the sun, on the statue at the origin of all this! He had come to Iona with a coin, so he needed another one to leave again, of the right size and with a hole in the middle!

Sam stuffed the precious coin in the robe the housekeeper monk had furnished him. The Colm Cille beach was less than ten minutes away. If he could only reach the stone . . .

He judged the natural chimney rising through the cave's ceiling to be at least thirty feet high. He had done a little rock climbing while he was on vacation, so he ought to be able to manage it; the main thing he needed was a leg up. Sam stowed the books safely at the very back of the grotto, then carefully stacked the tables one on top of another. From the top of this makeshift ladder, he was able to climb into the rock chimney without too much trouble, using handholds on either side. He slowly rose up the crack, trying to ignore the shouts of the Viking struggling outside the rockfall blocking the entrance. Finally Sam squeezed through a crack and emerged at the top of the hill. He eagerly filled his lungs with the salt air. Now all he had to do was be discreet.

Crawling on his belly like a lizard, he reached the opposite side of the hillock. Unless the Viking also climbed to the top of the hill, he would have little chance of spotting Sam. Still, Sam waited until he was a good distance away from the hill before he stood up. His goal: Colm Cille's cove.

Once he reached the grassy slope above the beach, Sam threw himself among the rocks. The stone statue was still there. He was going to go home! Feverishly he pulled the coin from his robe and set it into the recess shaped like the sun. The stone began to grow warmer; the terrible heat gripped his arm. Sam cried out . . .

. . . but no one could hear him scream.

CHAPTER FIVE

At the Front Lines

"Ahhhrrg!"

Sam's scream stuck in his throat as he vomited up the contents of his stomach. He was again on all fours on the muddy ground. The monks' golden coin hadn't brought him home!

When he could breathe again, he stood up, being careful not to get his tunic and pants too dirty. His heavy robe seemed to have disappeared. It was cool and foggy, like a spring morning, and he found himself in the middle of what must have been a village once. All that remained of the main street were skeletons of walls, crushed roofs, twisted scraps of iron, and collapsed beams. He looked for the stone statue. It was standing at the foot of an old fountain, half buried in weeds. And the coin was gone.

Where had he landed this time — and *when*? Even though the houses were in ruins, they had real doors and windows, not at all the style of the huts on Iona. But they weren't modern buildings either. Sam entered a house at random. Inside, scorched furniture and pieces of chairs were scattered over what remained of the mud-covered tiles. He rummaged for food in an old trunk, but without success. He stepped out of the house, went into another, and then a third. They were all devastated. He eventually reached the end of the street. The landscape around him wasn't any more engaging: a bleak, muddy plateau, where all the trees seemed to have been flattened by a terrible storm. He much preferred the view of the Atlantic on Iona.

"Here . . . over here . . ."

Sam jumped. A weak, disembodied voice could be heard from somewhere beyond a half-demolished shed.

It spoke again. "Is there . . . Is anyone there?"

Sam judged it best not to answer, but he walked toward the voice, through a garden that had been so thoroughly destroyed it looked almost like the surface of the moon. The voice was coming from a bramble-choked ravine.

"Please . . ."

A man was lying at the bottom of the ravine: a soldier. His uniform was encrusted with mud, and one of his legs was bent underneath him at an odd angle. He looked as if he had lost a lot of blood. Only his eyes stood out in the dirt that covered his face. "Please . . . something to drink. . . . Water."

The soldier's accent seemed strangely familiar to Sam. His clothes and his round helmet did too. He climbed cautiously down the ravine, especially wary of the brambles, as all he wore on his feet were his prehistoric flip-flops. He freed the metal canteen caught in the branches nearby, unscrewed it, and lifted it to the soldier's parched mouth. The man drank for a long time before he had his fill.

"Thanks," he said in a stronger voice. "The good Lord sent you. I . . . don't know what you're doing around here, or dressed like that, but you have to get the medics for me."

Sam nodded so as not to interrupt the man, who appeared to be on the verge of unconsciousness.

"You have to . . . go out the other end of the village. Follow the road without letting anyone see you. Just go straight ahead. Fort Souville is one kilometer away. But you must know that, right? Tell them . . ." He coughed weakly. "Tell them Corporal Chartrel of the . . . 239th Infantry Regiment is wounded. At Fleury, behind the Grange-aux-Morts. They'll understand . . . I don't know why the stretcher bearers didn't pick me up. I must have passed out." He looked at Sam beseechingly. "You'll do that, won't you? You won't leave me here, will you? I . . . I can't hang on much longer, you know."

Sam nodded.

"Good . . . I . . . above all, stay on the road, boy. And don't go up on the ridges, they're full of Germans." He seemed as if he were about to add something else, but then he closed his eyes and moaned softly.

There wasn't a minute to lose. Sam got himself out of the ravine and ran down the main street in the other direction. The war . . . It was a war, but which one? "Germans," the soldier had said, so was it World War II? Sam had a couple of fairly realistic period video games and he didn't recognize the man's uniform. No, it was more likely to be World War I. One day in history class they had shown a black-and-white film about the trenches and all that . . . yes, World War I. Chartrel was probably a French corporal.

Sam headed down the road bent double. He was almost

getting used to all this running, except that his white shirt and pants now made him a perfect target. And given the shattered trees and the ruined houses, he seemed to be in the middle of the battlefield.

He crossed the uniformly gray and desolate countryside without any problem. No Germans were in sight on the hills. Maybe it was still too early. Were there "war hours," the way there were business hours in an office?

"Halt! Who goes there?"

Three soldiers suddenly burst from a thicket and blocked his way, pointing their rifles at him.

"What's this, Marcel?" asked the tallest soldier, who wore a bewildered expression. "Do I shoot or don't I shoot?"

"Don't shoot, Jeannot," said the oldest one. "First, we have to know what's happening."

"*Saperlotte!* It looks like a boy!" exclaimed the third, who sported an impressive mustache.

"Who are you?" asked the oldest man. "Where did you come from?"

"I've come from Corporal Chartrel of the 239th Infantry Regiment," said Sam all at once. "He's over there in the village of Fleury, behind the Grange-aux-Morts, and his leg's hurt. I think he's in bad shape."

"Impossible — Chartrel! He was listed as missing in action the day before yesterday! How could he still be alive?"

"And how would you know that, kid?" asked the oldest one. "How can we tell you aren't some Kraut trick to draw us into an ambush?"

"So what do we do, then?" the tall one asked. "Do I shoot or not?"

"Lower your rifle, Jeannot!" urged the mustache. "He's just a kid! He speaks French and he knows the corporal!"

"*Maybe* he knows the corporal," Marcel retorted, "but it's not up to us to decide. We'll go tell the captain." He gestured with his chin at Sam. "Walk ahead of us, fellow, and don't try any tricks."

Sam obeyed without a word — he had learned the virtues of silence on Iona — but he couldn't help wondering what kind of soldiers he had run into. Apparently the big stupid one was on his first patrol and desperately wanted to break in his weapon.

"What about that crow over there, Marcel? Can I shoot it?"

"You idiot! Do you want the Germans to spot us? Don't worry, you'll have plenty of chances to make sparks fly if they send you to Douaumont!"

They continued their discussion until they reached Fort Souville, a large concrete pillbox overlooking the road and the town below. They entered it through a tunnel, greeting the guard in his sentry box.

"When are you coming to relieve me, Jeannot?" asked the guard.

"I haven't shot yet!" the big dummy answered, as if it were the most important thing in his life. They took a series of underground passageways — whose pattern Sam tried to memorize — to a break room, also underground, where soldiers were smoking, joking, and playing cards. Marcel rushed over to one of them, who was standing ramrod straight and coolly observing the activity around him.

"Captain!" cried Marcel, snapping to attention. "We captured a boy on the Fleury road! He claims to have seen Corporal Chartrel alive!"

The captain looked Sam over before saying, in an icy tone: "Take him to my office."

One of the soldiers immediately left his card game and escorted Sam to a room with dirty yellow walls, lit by two bare electric bulbs. Its only furniture was a table, three chairs, and a bookshelf.

The captain joined them ten minutes later. "Leave us, Châtaigner. I'll interrogate him myself."

When they were alone, the captain sat Sam down and stood across from him, both hands on the back of a chair.

"I could have you shot right away," he said without preamble. "You are in a forbidden zone. All the towns around here have been evacuated, even Verdun. Any civilian who appears in the area is automatically suspected of being a spy."

He watched to see the effect this had, but Sam was careful not to bat an eye.

"I don't have much time for you, boy. The Germans have become more and more dangerous in the last couple of weeks, and they could launch an offensive at any moment. Given the situation, no one is going to wonder whether I have sufficient reason for executing you."

He walked around Sam to look him in the face.

"For the time being, I can see only two possibilities. One: The patrol I just sent comes back safe and sound with Corporal Chartrel, and I'll just view you as a foolish young runaway. Perhaps you've escaped from an orphanage, which would explain your pajamas. If so, I'll turn you over to the police tomorrow and all you'll get is a good chewing-out. Or two: My patrol falls into a trap. In that case I'll consider you a traitor, with the consequences you can imagine."

"I really talked to the corporal —" Sam started.

The captain cut him off. "I don't care what you have to say, boy, and I have better things to do than grill you. Châtaigner is going to put you in a cell, and later on, we'll see. When he brings you back here, you'd better be telling me the truth. Otherwise . . ."

The captain grabbed Sam by his collar and heaved him toward the door. "Châtaigner, stick this idiot where he can cool his heels. Give him a blanket and something to eat. As soon as the detachment gets back, have the officer in charge report to me."

Two hours passed, or three; Sam lost all sense of time. He bundled himself up in an ugly brown blanket and devoured even the last crumbs of biscuit in his mess tin. His cell reeked of humidity and urine, but at least he wasn't cold. Above all, he prayed that the patrol would make it back to the fort without any harm. If by bad luck it ran into trouble . . . he didn't really believe the captain's threats. He couldn't just shoot a fourteen-year-old boy, even in wartime. On the other hand, Sam absolutely had to avoid being taken to a police station. The stone statue was very close to here, less than a mile away. If they sent him to the rear, to an orphanage or something, he might never get back to his own time. So he had to find a way to . . .

The big bolt crashed back, and the friendly mustachioed man who had captured him earlier stood framed in the doorway.

"How's it going, boy? Whew, it smells down here, doesn't it? What can I say? This is the hole, it's no place for you! Come on, on your feet. I'm taking you out to get some fresh air. There's someone who wants to talk to you."

Sam followed with his blanket. "Getting some fresh air" was

just an expression, because they actually went down the same blind passageways as on the way in, passed the break room, and stopped at a steel double door. Though he had convinced himself of the emptiness of the captain's threats, Sam half expected to emerge into a courtyard, facing a firing squad.

"Is . . . is the captain there?" he asked somewhat nervously.

"The captain? Oh, you'll see the captain soon enough!"

The man with the big mustache turned the door handle and gestured for him to go in. "I'll wait for you here, boy. Smoking's not allowed inside, and I wouldn't mind rolling myself a cigarette."

Sam took a step inside, and recognized the smell of a hospital. A dozen wounded men, some of them asleep, lay in the beds lining the walls.

A male nurse in a white coat gave Sam a big smile. "Léonard is over there, boy. He wants to thank you!"

Sam nervously approached the white screen and behind it found—Corporal Chartrel! He was lying on a gray sheet, his leg hidden under a kind of mesh frame. His face was pale and his features worn, but still Sam figured he couldn't be more than twenty-five or thirty. He welcomed Sam with a pained smile.

"Thanks . . . thanks, boy. You came just in the nick of time, you know. A little longer . . . I took a hit, two days ago, in the battle for Fleury, and slipped into the ravine. It saved me, in a way, but without you . . . Do you have a name, by the way?"

Sam searched for a first name that would sound French. "Jacques. I'm called Jacques."

"Well, Jacques, you're my guardian angel. The guys told me that you had to deal with the captain, but don't worry, we'll

47

help you. After what happened . . ." He stretched his arm out to Sam and slowly opened his fist. "Here. This is what I wanted to give you: my good-luck coin. I picked it up in a trench last year. Since nobody claimed it . . ."

Into Sam's open palm he dropped a silver medal with a hole in the center. The blue metal rim was inscribed RÉPUBLIQUE FRANÇAISE.

"It's the Médaille Militaire, boy. Only the bravest get it. Maybe I'll get one myself, who knows? The guy it belonged to must have lost the central medallion, or maybe it got shot out. . . . The way it is, it's not worth anything, but I thought it would protect me. You've got to hang on to something when you're under fire. And the proof it's good luck is that you came along."

The corporal was staring at Sam as intensely as Brother Ranald had the day before, almost as if he thought Sam had supernatural powers. But he had just gone down to the basement!

"Take it, boy. You deserve it!"

Sam closed his fingers over the medal. It was warm — was it the warmth of the corporal's hands, or something else? He now had the coin that would allow him to leave, he knew it. He didn't know where that certainty came from, *but he knew it!*

At that precise moment, a siren in the fort wailed out a warning, loud enough to blow out eardrums. Shouts echoed down the hallways: "Alert, alert! Attack! Attack! Everyone to their battle stations!"

Sam heard an explosion in the distance, muffled by the thickness of the walls. Then another one, a few seconds later.

"Those rats!" exclaimed the nurse as he took off his jacket.

"They never leave us in peace!" He headed for the door, grabbing a bag on the way. "Stay here, boy. This could take a while. I'm going to see if somebody needs me."

All the wounded men were now sitting up in bed and talking. The ceiling light dimmed.

"They must have hit the electricity," sighed the corporal.

They heard three more explosions, and then the bulbs briefly went out. At the next barrage, the infirmary was plunged into total darkness. Sam knew he might not get another chance.

"Thank you," he murmured, squeezing Chartrel's wrist.

He grabbed his blanket and rushed to the door. As best he could remember, the entrance to the fort was three long passageways from there, on the left. He began to run, touching the wall from time to time with his hand. Twice, he was almost bowled over by soldiers coming the other way in the darkness.

"To the bunker! Fast!"

Sam might have taken a wrong turn at the last junction if he hadn't seen daylight in the distance. The explosions were coming more often now, some of them very close, shaking the ground. He wondered how he would convince the guard to let him leave the fort. He flattened himself against the wall and observed the sentry box. Jeannot, the big dumb one, was on guard alone.

"Hey, Jeannot!" cried Sam, stepping away from the wall. "The captain sent me to get you!"

"What's that?" said the man, pointing his rifle at Sam.

"It's coming down hard at the bunker," continued Sam. "They need everybody!"

"At the bunker?"

"That's right! The captain needs all of the shooters right now!"

"The shooters," Jeannot murmured, lowering his rifle. "You mean I'm going to shoot?"

"If you hurry, yes! The Germans aren't going to wait for you!"

"But . . . what about standing guard?"

"The captain said to just close the gate. I'll take care of it. Go ahead!"

The big oaf hesitated for a few seconds, just long enough for his brain to grasp what was happening. "I'm going to shoot my rifle!" he said, looking ecstatic. "I'm going to shoot!"

He rushed into the underground passage. Sam shook his head. With soldiers like that, this war wouldn't be won any time soon!

Once Jeannot disappeared down the passageway, Sam approached the gate. The shelling was increasing outside, raising enormous clouds of dust. This was no time for a stroll, but he really didn't have any choice: If a shell wound up hitting the stone statue, he could say good-bye to his own time.

He waited until the next explosion, then did a hundred-yard dash toward the Fleury road. The air was full of shrapnel and noise, with occasional flashes of light streaking the sky overhead. Sam covered himself with his blanket, hoping that it would hide him a little. The detonations now sounded both before and behind him, accompanied by the rattle of rifle fire. The Fort Souville artillery must be shooting back. Jeannot would be in seventh heaven!

Just when Sam thought he had gotten through the most dangerous area, he heard a bullet whistle past his ear. He'd been spotted! He threw himself to the ground and rolled into a ditch for cover. He waited there, trying to calm down. . . . No more firing. After a couple of minutes, he began to crawl on his belly like a snake, protected by the earthen bank. And what if the Germans had also taken Fleury? He glanced quickly toward the town. No, the way was open.

After two hundred yards of crawling, he finally reached the first ruined building. Leaning against what was left of a chimney, he realized that he was black with mud from head to foot — a professional camouflage job! Behind him, on the other side of the road, the guns on the ridges pounded the fort, the deadly fire raining endlessly from the sky. . . . It was nothing like in the movies.

When Sam was feeling a little braver, he scuttled silently from house to house, being careful not to show himself. The old half-demolished fountain hadn't moved, nor had the stone statue in the weeds.

He took the corporal's medal and squeezed it very hard against his heart. "Please, please — take me home."

With a shaking hand, Sam stretched out the medal to the stone statue.

CHAPTER SIX

Alone in the Dark

Sam felt the cold ground under his hands and knees. He was bent double with nausea, but he was better able to control his spasms and didn't need to vomit. On the other hand, he was in total darkness. Could the lamp in the basement have gone out after his departure? Sam stood up, arms outstretched, and groped for a wall. He found it two steps in front of him, as smooth and cold as the ground — certainly not the wall of the bookstore.

A wave of anxiety swept over him. What if he was trapped? What if the stone had taken him to a place with no way out? Or what if he had become blind? Time travel must have horrible effects on the body. . . . In a panic, he turned like a caged animal. The room wasn't very big, four yards by four, with a massive stone block in the center. But it didn't have any door. Could there be an exit above him? He jumped into the air a few times, but he wasn't able to reach the ceiling.

Sam climbed onto the big stone block and reached up on tiptoe. Something soft brushed his fingertips, and he yanked on it. A rope — better yet, a rope ladder, anchored somewhere high above. He grabbed the first rung, swung himself up, and began to climb. The anchor seemed to hold. He ascended cautiously, to avoid twisting the ladder, till he reached a square opening at the top. This let him into a low hallway that was also completely dark.

Sam crawled forward on all fours, feeling the ground around him — a wise move, because after turning into a wider passage, he suddenly felt the floor fall away. There was a huge hole in the middle of the underground corridor. He had to stand up and slowly, very slowly, work his way around it, clinging to the wall, his feet searching out the ledge at the hole's rim. He then returned to hands and knees and resumed his progress.

At the next bend, it seemed to him that it wasn't so dark. Yes, there was a flickering light in the distance. He stood up and began to run. An oil lamp, in a room to the right . . .

"My God!" he exclaimed.

Hieroglyphics — hieroglyphics everywhere! And people in profile, painted in bright, glowing colors. Some carried jars, baskets of fruit, or fowl; others harvested wheat or played music. Next to the tiny oil lamp on the floor, a small tray held a wooden brush and earthen pots filled with pigments, as well as a sheaf of papyrus that no doubt served as a pattern, except that each sheet showed a series of identical drawings. He was in Egypt! Maybe in a pyramid!

Just then, he heard noises in the hallway: footsteps and whispers. Sam had just enough time to blow out the lamp.

"Did you accompany him to the courtyard?" a voice murmured.

"To the courtyard, as you ordered me, master. He must have headed for the temple before the workers returned."

The two people were speaking a singsong, pleasant-sounding language.

"Are you sure he doesn't suspect anything?"

"I'm sure of it. He toured the site as expected."

"He didn't mention the objects he wanted to store with the sarcophagus?"

"Not a word."

Sam could make out the dancing flames of a torch. The two men were coming his way.

"Too bad. We will have to act before the chamber is sealed."

"The funeral won't take place before the next decan, master."

"I know that!" the first man answered sharply. "That's why I chose the date. The full moon will be in five days. He will have to go to the pool at the Temple of Ramses for the ritual bath. At the sixth hour of the night, station one of your men on the wall. A single arrow should be enough."

Their gliding steps stopped near the door. Sam could see the light from their torch on the back wall: A huge falcon-headed god with a single eye was staring at him. If the two plotters decided to enter . . .

"What then, master?"

"I want your accomplice to disappear. I'll take care of the rest."

"And . . ." The second speaker hesitated. "What about the payment?"

"You will each get six bags of wheat and six of barley, as agreed."

They must have turned around, because their voices began to fade away in the other direction.

"Can you guarantee the discretion of your men?"

"Yes, master. They know what they risk if they betray me."

"The agitation by the workers will serve us; the vizier will be distracted. Do you think there will be a revolt?"

"I don't know, master. The men have been restless for the last few days, and . . ."

Sam could no longer make out what they were saying: The pounding of his heart drowned out their whispers. He remained frozen in the corner until he could feel the blood flowing through his veins again. A sarcophagus . . . the Temple of Ramses . . . he was indeed in the age of the pyramids!

When he couldn't hear any more sounds, he prepared to leave his hiding place. Going back the way he'd come would serve no purpose. He would follow the hallway in hopes of finding a way out — and try to do so before the workers resumed their jobs!

On hands and knees once again, Sam groped his way to the foot of a staircase. He climbed about fifteen steps and came out on a floor lit by the same kind of oil lamp he had seen earlier. The hallway was magnificent, its ceiling painted with a starry sky, its walls decorated with a huge golden boat pulled by a crowd of servants. In the middle of the boat, a man with a rich headdress — the pharaoh? — was holding the hands of two gods, one with a dog's head and one with a ram's. Sam was sorry that he hadn't paid more attention in class: Anubis, Thoth, Horus . . . a jumble of names came to him, but he couldn't remember which was which. He also noticed that he wasn't able to read the hieroglyphics: His built-in translator had its limits.

The hallway split in two and Sam decided to go to the left. He climbed another flight of stairs and could feel heat weighing heavily on his shoulders. Not a bad sign . . . five more steps, and he could see sunlight at the end of the corridor and up another flight of stairs, twenty feet away. He took off his shirt and knotted it over his pants, as the heat was becoming unbearable. The doorway wasn't very high and seemed to open onto a perfect blue sky. But just then a jumble of shouts rose from outside:

"You don't have the right!" a man yelled hoarsely. "You're under the vizier's orders!"

"You'll see if we have the right," somebody shouted back. "We haven't been paid in two decans!"

"Yes! Yes!" a chorus of voices agreed.

A whip cracked.

"If the Left team refuses to go to the valley again," the hoarse voice continued, "I will refer them directly to the vizier!"

"Give him my best regards!" the second voice shot back. "And you can tell him my team and I are going home as soon as this tomb is finished. We aren't starting another work site until we're paid what we're owed! And we're talking full weight and full measure!"

The crowd rumbled its approval.

"In that case, the vizier will authorize me to use force!" the hoarse voice threatened.

"Just try, scribe! If you break our arms and wrists, you can paint the rooms yourself!"

There was a shout of laughter; the argument seemed to have hit its mark. A figure strode furiously into the doorway, a black silhouette against the blue sky. Sam quickly backed into a dark room.

"Since you're so clever, Peneb," the man in the doorway said, "will you explain why you haven't finished Setni's tomb?"

A second figure appeared in the doorway, carrying a torch. "We ran out of paint, as you know very well, scribe. Your suppliers apparently miscalculated the amount that would be necessary."

"This tomb belongs to a priest, not a prince of the blood. You should have worked faster!"

The two voices were now coming down the stairs. Sam was sure of it.

"Setni was the best priest of Amon that Egypt has known for generations. He must be honored in death the way he was in life."

"You think yourself able to judge a priest's quality, Peneb? And to decide how much time should be spent on his tomb?"

The footsteps were now very close, and the torch made the hallway as bright as day.

"Apparently his son paid you generously for our work, scribe. You and the whole Institution of the Tomb."

"The Institution's accounts don't concern you, Peneb. And you should be careful not to provoke me and my staff. Your workers would do better to shorten their breaks and be sure that . . ."

The torch suddenly lit the room where Sam had taken refuge. Two black eyes glared in at him. They belonged to a man with a shaved head, wearing a loincloth and carrying a whip.

"WHAT ABOUT THIS?" the man screamed. "WHAT IS THIS?"

Without giving Sam time to open his mouth, he violently whipped him on the thigh.

"A little thief in *your* tomb, Peneb!"

Crack! Another lash of the whip, whose bite drew a cry from Sam. The scribe was beside himself.

"I will tell the vizier how you care for Setni's tomb, mark my words! Any robber or runaway servant can . . ."

He raised his hand to crack the whip a third time, but Peneb stepped forward. "Stop that right away, scribe! If you want to get angry at somebody, take it out on me!"

The two men stood face to face. The scribe's features twisted in hatred. "Can you tell me what this intruder is doing at *your* work site, Peneb?"

The other man didn't even blink. "He's my nephew, scribe. He's here to learn the work. And in the future I advise you not to touch him."

They continued glaring at each other. Then the scribe spun on his heels, shoving aside the curious workers gathered by the door.

"The vizier is watching you," he thundered. "The whole team of the Left! Remember that!"

The silence that followed lasted well after the scribe's departure. The men in the doorway looked steadily at Sam. Most were no taller than he was. They were swarthy, toughened by their work, their arms and legs dusted with fine white powder. These were workers who slaved to earn their living by the sweat of their brows, the kind of people who must have existed everywhere and in every time. . . .

Finally one of them smiled and said, "Well, Peneb, aren't you going to welcome your nephew?"

A few of the workers applauded, and Peneb helped Sam to his feet. The foreman then assigned each worker a job, and led Sam to an antechamber where he himself was carving a mural in low relief. Without a word, he gestured to him to sit down, and went back to work by lamplight, as if nothing had happened. With a fine chisel and a mallet, he carved in figures that had been drawn on the wall earlier, using a huge grid pattern. Four-fifths of the mural was already carved; the image he was finishing now showed a life-size figure who was receiving a gift from a god with the head of a heron, or some other animal with a long curved beak. Fascinated, sweltering in the heat, not daring to move because his thigh was on fire, Sam watched as Peneb skillfully shaped the stone, bringing out the folds of a garment or the curve of an arm with a few subtle strokes of the chisel.

Three full hours passed this way before Peneb spoke, rousing Sam from a gentle torpor.

"You've put me in a difficult situation, boy. The scribe will warn the guards to keep an eye on us. The workers who go into the tombs are sworn to secrecy, and if you disappear today I'll be asked about it. You're going to have to stay with me for a while, or else they'll suspect that I lied. And the scribe is just waiting for an excuse to fire me."

Peneb paused for a moment — he was carving the main figure's eye — before continuing.

"This is Setni, the high priest of Amon. He died two months ago. When the embalmers finish their work, his mummy will be put in the sarcophagus. I hope you didn't come here to locate his tomb and rob it."

For the first time that afternoon, he looked directly at Sam. "You're running away, aren't you? They beat you, or didn't give you enough to eat? I've seen plenty of little servants like you who wanted to escape their masters. Rich people enjoy their wealth only when they're surrounded by poor ones! Pah!"

He spat contemptuously on the floor, then started work on the gift that the heron-headed god was holding out. From time to time he consulted a papyrus that showed the design of the mural.

"What's your name, boy?"

"Sam," he said, with a bizarre accent.

"*Sem?* Well, you may as well learn something, Sem. You have to handle the chisel delicately and know exactly where to set it. The eye must be able to see not only the place where the hand strikes, but the effect to be achieved by it. Here, like this." With a few blows, Peneb brought out the beginnings of a sun. "The duty of the sculptor is to give eternity to the shape he sculpts, do you understand? The painters then give it life with their colors."

As Peneb spoke, Sam was astonished to see that he was sketching out a tall object that was rounded on top and had a sun with six rays in its center. It was a simplified but perfectly recognizable image of the stone statue. *Setni the priest had owned the stone statue!*

Sam thought he was going to be sick.

"Excuse me. What . . . what does this scene mean?"

Peneb didn't answer immediately. He was carefully making a series of closely spaced cuts to indicate the cavity at the base of the statue.

"Setni would greet his guests here in the antechamber. The dead like to be portrayed at important times in their lives. Clearly, the god Thoth is giving him an object that must have mattered to him."

"Do you know what it is?"

"No idea. His son gave us the design in accordance with Setni's wishes. Priests of Amon sometimes make demands that we can't fathom."

"Then Setni's son must know about it?"

"I wouldn't be too sure. We talked about it when the work began, and he wasn't able to tell me exactly what this object was. I would guess that it's a sacred vase — upside down, perhaps. But for what reason . . ."

"Is it significant that it's the god Thoth who is giving him the present?"

Peneb nodded in approval. "You've got a good brain for a servant boy. The choice of Thoth is never an accident. You know as well as I do that ibis-headed Thoth is the patron of magicians, doctors, and scribes — as well as the master of time, of course, and the juggler of days and seasons. That doesn't shed much light on the object, does it? But it's good that you have a curious mind. Come along," he added, standing up. "I'm finished with the antechamber. Let's go tell the painters they can take over."

Sam followed him in a daze. "Thoth, the master of time," he repeated to himself. "The juggler of days and seasons!"

CHAPTER SEVEN

The Million-Year Palace

After a few days in Egypt, Sam could almost imagine he was on some kind of foreign-exchange program. Several of his friends had been to Europe during their vacations to improve their knowledge of German or Italian, though they mainly improved their knowledge of girls, music, and cigarettes. So why not Egypt instead of Germany or Italy? Aside from the fact that he and his host family were born three or four thousand years apart. . . .

They turned out to be charming. Peneb's wife, Nout, accepted him as her favorite nephew without asking a single question. On the evening of his arrival, she asked her two young sons, Didou and Biatou, whose favorite occupation was to run around laughing, to help him wash in the small pond in the garden. Then she fixed dinner: dried fish with chopped cucumbers and onions, followed by grapes and honey cakes — a much more appetizing menu than the daily fare at Iona. At bedtime she rolled out a mat for him on the house rooftop. The air was soft and scented, and Sam slept better than he had since he left his own bedroom. He had no complaints about the lodging or hospitality.

Where scheduled activities were concerned, however, his foreign exchange organization had been less inspired. That was because the village of Set Maat was practically a walled camp, carefully watched by the *medjay*, the local police. Because the men decorated the royal tombs, which were filled with valuables, the Institution of the Tomb feared that they would reveal specifics about the treasures to grave robbers. As a result, the villagers didn't go out much, except to go to the work sites. There was even a servant class that carried out all of the tasks that would have brought the workers in contact with the outside world: fishing, shopping, washing clothes, carrying water, and so on. Thus the people of Set Maat spent most of their time in one another's company, paying visits, organizing evenings of singing and dancing, or arranging tournaments of a checkers-like game that Sam was unable to master. Didou and Biatou explained the rules to him, but Sam always lost his pieces by his fifth or sixth turn, which the two children found hilarious.

As a result, Sam was able to go on only a single outing during his visit. Very early one morning, when Peneb had already left for the work site, Nout came to wake him up.

"Sem, do you want to come to the Thebes market with me?"

"The Thebes market?"

"I know the *medjay* on duty today; they will let us through."

Sam didn't hesitate long: A market meant shopping, and shopping meant money, and money meant coins. And coins meant . . .

He put on the loincloth that Nout had loaned him, and joined her as she prepared her two baskets. With Didou and Biatou, who frolicked around naked, they passed through the village gate without any trouble, especially after Nout gave the two guards a package of honey cakes. They then walked to a wharf and boarded a long oar boat to cross the Nile, where the traffic was as dense as a highway at rush hour. The village of Set Maat was located on the west bank of the river, called the Bank of the Dead. Besides the workers' village, it held only the pharaohs' huge palaces and a steep cliff into which the tombs were dug. As far as visiting pyramids, Sam was out of luck; Peneb told him that none had been built in a very long time — too expensive — and the ones that already existed stood far to the north. Another black mark against the foreign exchange organization.

As they neared the opposite bank, the Bank of the Living, Sam was dazzled by Thebes's beauty. The city stretched along the river for several miles, luxurious neighborhoods alternating with imposing monuments and clusters of narrow alleys, in an attractive sweep of sandy yellow structures. The market, which was held in the shadow of the great Temple of Amon, was jammed with people yelling and shoving amid dozens of stands overflowing with fruit, flowers, colored pottery, clucking fowl, and cloths of all sorts. Nout knew exactly what she wanted and moved easily among the crowds and the donkeys. She bought this measure of figs from that merchant, that bunch of leeks from another, and would buy her coriander only from an old Nubian woman with a wrinkled face. To his dismay, Sam quickly realized that nobody in the market paid with money. They all bartered their products, after complex negotiations that allowed Nout, for example, to swap four homemade honey cakes for a jar of goose fat or wax. The Thebans didn't use coins at all! They didn't even know they existed!

"Are you feeling all right, Sem?"

His gaze had strayed to the impressive wall of the Temple of Amon. "I was just wondering . . . Setni was the high priest at the Temple of Amon, right?"

She nodded, gesturing at him to speak more softly.

Sam had just had an idea. "And Setni's son, do you know him?"

"Only by name. He is called Ahmosis."

"I suppose he lives in Thebes?"

"Yes, in a beautiful house near the Montou estate."

"Could you . . . could you take me there?"

Nout frowned. "Certainly not. For one thing, I don't know exactly where it is. And even if I did, his servants would never let us in. You're hoping to get yourself another job as a household servant, is that it?"

Sam made a vague gesture.

"I must remind you, Sem, that Peneb still needs you. If you don't come back to the village today, the Institution scribe could cause him problems. Wait another day or two!"

Nout turned out to be right. They hadn't been back from Thebes for more than an hour before the scribe burst into the foreman's house, escorted by two guards.

Nout faced him without the least embarrassment. "Are you looking for Peneb, scribe?"

"No. I wanted to see you."

"Me?"

"You. A wife has ways of persuading her husband that the Institution does not. You have to talk Peneb out of leading this revolt."

"The revolt? But the men's revolt is just, scribe! We haven't received our rations for nearly a month!"

"That's not the point. I have spoken with the vizier; the granaries are empty. We have to wait for wheat and barley to arrive from the north. Two decans, three at the most. The Institution can't do anything until then."

"The granaries are empty, but the priests and the scribes eat well enough! Here in the village we have exhausted our reserves. If we weren't able to fend for ourselves —" Nout began.

"A revolt won't do anyone any good, Nout. Your husband could lose his job and so could many of his workers. What will you do if the Institution fires him?"

"Peneb is the best sculptor in Thebes, and his men are among the most skillful in all Egypt. It would take the Institution years to replace them."

"Perhaps," the scribe admitted. "But are you prepared to run that risk? What is the best sculptor in Thebes worth if he doesn't have a roof over his head and his children are begging in the streets? I'm told you have two charming boys, Nout. Think about it."

He turned around on the threshold. "By the way, how is Peneb's young nephew working out?"

Sam, who was on the terrace and hadn't missed a word of the conversation, felt a dry lump in his throat.

"I don't think he's very talented," answered Nout. "And he's not a very hard worker. Peneb is already thinking of sending him back to his brother in Memphis."

"I suspected as much," the scribe said with a nasty chuckle. "He looked like a weakling to me, with that pale, sick-looking skin of his. If he needs a couple of lashes to get his blood moving, bring him to me."

The scribe's visit did nothing to calm the tensions with the Institution. The next day Peneb came back from his job site unusually early, accompanied by a half dozen of his companions. They were all very excited.

"Setni's tomb is finished," he declared, setting his tool bag on a trunk. "We're stopping work."

"You're stopping?" asked Nout incredulously.

"We talked it over and we all agree. We won't do anything more until new food supplies arrive. And the Right crew thinks the same way."

"Better yet, we've decided to complain to the palace," added a worker who was built like a wrestler. "At my house, there isn't a drop of beer in the jars, and what water remains is stagnant. My little girl is only three, and she cries every night because she's thirsty and hungry!"

"Mesou is right," said another. "We have to demand what's due us at the Temple of Ramses. If we just sit around here, nothing will happen!"

"Yes!" they all chorused. "To the Temple of Ramses! To the Million-Year Palace!"

The Temple of Ramses! Where had Sam heard that phrase before? He suddenly remembered the conversation he'd overheard in Setni's tomb: "The full moon will be in five days," the mysterious voice had murmured. "He will have to go to the pool at the Temple of Ramses for the ritual bath. At the sixth hour of the night, station one of your men on the wall. A single arrow should be enough."

As the workers' excitement built, Sam approached Nout. "Ahmosis, the son of Setni — he wouldn't happen to be a priest at the Temple of Ramses, would he?"

Nout nodded and turned away to get something for her guests to eat and drink. Sam's mind was spinning. Who could this "he" be that they were planning to assassinate, this "he" who would come to inspect Setni's tomb, if not Ahmosis, Setni's own son? Ahmosis, who was a priest in the Temple of Ramses, whose duties might require him to perform a ritual on the night of the full moon? Ahmosis, who might know something about the stone statue?

Sam counted his fingers feverishly: He'd been in Egypt one, two, three, four, *five* days. Exactly five days! He had to warn Ahmosis.

Should he tell Peneb and his friends? What if one of the plotters happened to be among the Set Maat workers? In that case, Sam wouldn't survive very long. No, it was best to take advantage of the strike to get into the palace and somehow try to meet Ahmosis. It was only a couple of hours until nightfall.

The news of the march to the Temple of Ramses gradually spread through the village. The workers from both groups — the Left and Right crews — gathered on the square and talked things over. Finally they picked up their tools and set off in the direction of the Temple, flanked by the women and children and improvising slogans on the way.

"The vizier must hear us out!"

"Our children are hungry!"

"No more parley, we want barley!"

As they made their way along, waving their pickaxes and hatchets, Sam discreetly put some questions to one of Peneb's neighbors.

"I've never been to the Temple of Ramses. Do you know what it looks like?"

"Of course! I even helped decorate it. Ramses had it built so the greatness of his reign would be celebrated while he was alive as well as for eternity! Hence the name 'Million-Year Palace.' A tiny part of the riches stored there would be enough to feed the city of Thebes for a year!"

"I've heard that there are baths for the priests?"

"Have you been living under a rock, boy? Don't you honor the gods where you're from? Of course there are baths! They're off the right of the second courtyard, the one surrounded by hedges and flower beds. But if you're thinking of cooling yourself in there, you're making a big mistake. Only the Temple priests have access to those baths! And if you try to enter, they'll tan your hide, believe me."

The man's wife elbowed him and he started yelling with the others again: "Our children are hungry! We want wheat and barley!" Sam didn't dare pursue the subject.

Having marched for a quarter of an hour in the setting sunlight, the three hundred inhabitants of Set Maat reached what looked like a fortified castle. The walls were at least fifteen feet high, and soldiers with drawn bows stood in the watchtowers.

"We are the royal tomb workers," cried Peneb. "We have come to demand the pay we are owed for our work."

The guards had a moment of hesitation, followed by long discussions and stairs climbed and descended. Finally, after about twenty minutes, one of their leaders leaned over the crenellated wall.

"Set your tools down before the main gate," he said. "The Institution scribes will receive you."

A roar of satisfaction rose from the parade. The little troop passed through the first gate, then a second, and found itself before the monumental pillars of Ramses's mortuary temple, a gigantic mud-brick building. A dozen scribes met them there, torches in hand. They asked the demonstrators to designate five men as a formal delegation. This set off a new round of cries and protests, as some workers felt that all of the heads of families should be heard. Sam took advantage of the commotion to observe his surroundings. He was in the second courtyard, the one that Peneb's neighbor had mentioned, and the twilight was in his favor. Pathways led to the right and left, lined by hedges and flowers. The baths were surely very close. . . .

Sam allowed himself to fall to the back of the group and, while all eyes were on Peneb and the other volunteers, moved over to the nearest flower bed. A glance up at the watch-tower showed that no one was paying him any attention. He crouched against the hedge and forced his way into the tangle of branches, biting his lips against the twigs jabbing his flesh. There was no reaction from the soldiers. By sucking in his stomach, Sam was able to push through to the open space between the hedge and the wall. He then followed the wall to the end of the courtyard, stopping at the foot of a date palm whose fronds hid him from above. He couldn't see the courtyard anymore, but by spreading the leaves of the hedge, he could keep an eye on the pathway leading to the baths — assuming Peneb's neighbor hadn't made a mistake.

Now there was nothing to do but wait.

CHAPTER EIGHT

The Glass Scarab

A crunching on the gravel path . . .

Sam woke with a start. For a fraction of a second he wondered where he was. The Set Maat workers . . . the demonstration . . . the Million-Year Temple . . . everyone had left, including Peneb's delegation, and then . . . after a while, there hadn't been any noise. He must have fallen asleep. And now someone was walking on the path.

Sam peered out through the leaves of the hedge. The night was well along and the full moon, veiled by lacy clouds, cast a pale light. The sixth hour? Somewhere in the distance, the sound of a trumpet could be heard, and the footsteps were coming closer. Sam blinked to drive his sleepiness away. A shape . . . a man in a loincloth, his head shaved, carrying a rod topped by a torch. Was it Ahmosis?

The man approached the small door just on the other side of the flower beds and stuck his torch in the waiting bracket. He held a rod in his hand, which he inserted into a lock. The locking systems here were complicated, with a whole network of strings to untwist. The door opened and the priest disappeared, leaving the torch behind. That was a problem for Sam, who would have to cross the pool of light and risk attracting the guards' attention. But what else could he do? If he waited until Ahmosis came back out, it would be too late. If he called out to the priest, the soldiers would be on him before he had the time to explain himself. And Sam didn't especially care to have his hide tanned!

Holding his hands in front of his face, Sam pushed his way through the hedge, then dashed across the pool of light. The door was wide open; it would just take a single leap to get past the gravel, which would make noise underfoot. He gathered himself, jumped as far as possible, and landed without too much trouble in a flower bed with long-stemmed plants. They were papyri — more pleasant and less noisy than the gravel.

Slowly Sam stood up. He was now in a garden with bushes, reeds, and an earthen mound covered with trimmed grass. In the middle lay a large rectangular pool, three-quarters filled with water. The priest stood at the edge of the pool, hands clasped in front of him, murmuring something inaudible. Sam's legs began to twitch; he couldn't bring himself to approach. How could he introduce himself? What would he say?

The priest took the first step down into the pool. He stopped again and recited a second series of prayers. *Come on,* Sam told himself, *there isn't any choice. I have to get home!* He thought of his father and grandmother. *Come on! Be brave!*

It was then that Sam noticed a movement on the left-hand wall. A shadow appeared — a man sitting astride the wall. An archer.

"Watch out!" screamed Sam.

Something whistled through the air and the priest tumbled into the water. A second arrow immediately sliced into the ripples where his body had disappeared. Sam didn't know what to do.

"Help!" he yelled. "Help!"

Now the archer was aiming at him. Sam dove into the papyri and clearly heard an arrow slash through the stems above him. Flat on the ground, he was more or less protected, as long as the killer didn't decide to jump down into the garden. . . . Suddenly a bell rang, followed by a series of shouts and exclamations. The alarm had been raised.

Sam crawled through the papyri to see if anything was stirring over in the pool. Nothing. A procession of guards ran along the watchtower wall. Sam looked up; the archer had disappeared.

He burst out of his hiding place and ran toward the pool. Maybe Ahmosis was still alive! Without thinking, he jumped into the water at the very moment the priest was stepping out of it.

"What the . . . ?" breathed the priest.

"Sacrilege!" a voice above them cried. "A priest of Ramses is being attacked!"

Sam instantly realized the problems he had just created for himself.

"Release the priest at once!" the captain of the guards shouted down from the wall. Several soldiers had taken up positions around him.

"It wasn't me!" shouted Sam indignantly. "There was an

archer, up there where you are. He was the one who shot the arrow!"

But the guard captain paid no attention. "Ahmosis, are you all right? Did he hurt you?"

"No harm done, Mekhnat. You got here in time."

"Don't move," Mekhnat ordered. "I'm coming down with reinforcements. And you others: If this assassin tries to escape, run him through!"

Sam turned to the priest. "It wasn't me, I swear! I was hiding in the reeds! I saw the guy with the bow! I yelled to warn you!"

Ahmosis was wiping his dripping skull with surprising calm. He was clearly not wounded; his dive had saved him.

"You are in a sacred pool," he said without particular emotion. "Only the priests of Ramses are allowed to bathe here."

"It was a plot!" Sam burst out. "I overheard them the other day in Setni's tomb — your father's tomb! They were talking about the full moon and the Temple of Ramses. They were going to kill you at the sixth hour!" Sam's thoughts were getting mixed up and he was almost sobbing. "It wasn't me! I swear the archer was there! That's why I yelled!"

"Save your breath for the vizier," Mekhnat said as he entered the garden with his men. "Even if you have no chance of saving your skin. Seize him!"

Two soldiers rushed to grab Sam's wrists.

"He must have gotten in yesterday during the workers' demonstration," the captain continued. "I told you that you shouldn't have received them, Ahmosis."

"Priests must listen to the people," said Ahmosis. "Just as the Institution must keep its promises."

"Just the same, this boy could have killed you!"

"Captain," interrupted one of the soldiers. "I found this bow near the gate!"

Mekhnat grinned as he took the weapon in his hands. "This signs your death warrant, you little toad!"

"He must have thrown it away!" Sam cried. "You heard me, didn't you? I was the one who sounded the alarm!"

"Probably in hopes of fooling us!" Mekhnat shot back. "I even wonder . . ."

He leaned toward Ahmosis and said something in his ear. Sam caught only scraps of it: ". . . execute . . . now . . . so as not to bother . . . vizier."

That muttering! That way of whispering! Sam couldn't believe his ears. It was one of the two voices he'd heard in Setni's tomb! The one who answered in such a servile way, and kept saying "master" right and left. The head of the guards was part of the plot! That's why he wanted to get rid of Sam!

"It's . . . It's him!" he sputtered. "He was in the tomb! It's his voice, I recognize it!"

Mekhnat gave him a resounding slap.

"Dirty little liar!" he yelled. "You'll have to come up with some other story! Take him to the cells and clap him in irons! Immediately!"

Ahmosis took a step toward Sam with his hand raised, like a referee calling a foul. "Not so fast, Mekhnat. I am the pharaoh's priest, and the decision is mine."

"You aren't going to believe this little monkey, are you?"

"Lend me your torch, Mekhnat."

Mekhnat passed it to the priest, looking resentful. Ahmosis brought the torch close to Sam's face and examined him carefully. Then he spoke to the guards:

"Soldiers, continue searching the palace. The person we are looking for must still be hiding somewhere. As for this boy, you can release him. I know him and can vouch for him."

Sam lived through the following hours in a state of complete astonishment. After the altercation with Mekhnat, he was led to one of the rooms reserved for priests, in the west wing of the palace. It had a bed with a headrest, a bench with lion's feet for legs, two simple chairs, a table cluttered with papyri, and several chests. A guard with a sword protected the entryway, and Sam could see the first rays of the sun shooting through a high, tiny window. He had time then to think and turn the events of the night over in his mind. He had been so frightened! Everything had happened so quickly! He had thought all was lost, and then . . . what did Ahmosis mean by claiming to know him? And what fate was being prepared for him now?

Finally, after several hours, Ahmosis entered the room. He was still wearing his loincloth, but had put a white shawl around his shoulders and wore large rings on both hands. His gaze seemed all the more penetrating because his eyebrows were shaved and his eyes underlined with black. He dropped easily into one of the two chairs and nodded toward the other.

"Sit down, please. The time must have hung heavy on your hands. I apologize. I had to take care of a few problems."

"Have you arrested him?"

"The archer? No. But I suspect that it won't be long."

"Do you know who he is, then?"

"Perhaps. Mekhnat has disappeared."

"Mekhnat — disappeared?"

"He didn't report for the eighth-hour formation. He was supposed to gather the guard together to discuss the search. Everyone was surprised when he wasn't there."

"Do you think Mekhnat himself could have shot the arrows?"

"No, that would have been too risky. But one of his men has also deserted. I would deduce that Mekhnat bribed him to assassinate me."

Ahmosis reported all of this with a tranquil and benevolent air.

"There was someone else in the tomb when I overheard him," Sam said. "Mekhnat called him 'master,' as if he were more important than him."

"That is so. I wondered why they both insisted on accompanying me."

Sam wasn't following him. "I'm sorry?"

"My cousin Kamosis. He is a scribe with the Institution. The other day, he and Mekhnat insisted on coming to inspect my father's tomb. According to them, the workers weren't to be trusted and might have turned on me. Now I know better."

The scribe! The second voice belonged to the scribe! He was the one giving Mekhnat orders. He had arranged Ahmosis's murder!

"But if he's your cousin, why would he want to kill you?" Sam asked.

The priest smiled. "Probably for the same reasons that brought you here."

Sam turned beet red. "I . . . I don't know what . . ."

"Don't worry, my boy," said Ahmosis, patting him on the knee. "All this will remain between the two of us. My father told me about you."

"What?" Sam cried. "But that's impossible!"

"Not at all. Setni was no ordinary man. He was one of the greatest priests of Amon and the most trusted advisor to three successive pharaohs. He seemed able to . . ."

Ahmosis's voice was heavy with sadness.

"He seemed able to see what nobody else could see. To understand people that no one else could understand. At times he . . . he would go away. He would disappear one morning and come back in the evening, or a few days later, or a decan later, on occasion. He would bring back curious objects of unknown manufacture, made in countries so far away they had no name. He never explained how he had spent his time, whether he had traveled or simply run into merchant caravans. That was his secret."

Sam couldn't help but make the connection with his father. His heart tightened painfully.

"Didn't you . . . didn't you try to find out his secret?"

"Yes, of course! But he was more clever than I! When I was fifteen years old, we went to the top of the western hill, the one where the goddess Meretseger lives. I never forgot what he said to me then. 'You see,' he told me, pointing to the city and the river at our feet, 'that's where real life is. There, and only there. I know that you would like to follow me, Ahmosis. I am asking you not to do so. There are too many dangers and temptations, too much misery and sadness. Take a wife, have children, watch them grow up. Serve your gods and your pharaoh, cherish those around you. Nothing else deserves it, and nothing else is worth it. If you knew one hundredth of what I know, Ahmosis, nothing would mean anything to you anymore. Neither the past nor the future. You would have only what I have: a dusty present and the taste of infinite failure. And that is not what I want for my son.'"

The priest shrugged. "At the time his words seemed very strange to me. But there was so much seriousness in his voice and so much weariness in his eyes, I chose to take his advice."

Sam was fascinated. It was as if after walking endlessly in the darkness, after stumbling and running into unseen walls, he could glimpse a light very far in the distance—a fragile, flickering light, but a light just the same. He felt less alone.

"You said something earlier. . . . He knew me?"

Ahmosis nodded. "Yes. About two years ago he told me that you were going to come."

"That . . . that I was going to come?"

"'A light-skinned boy,' he said. 'Fourteen years old, with brown hair, blue eyes, and fine features, and a stubborn but determined expression. He may not know where he is, or perhaps *who* he is. But you must help him, because in his way, he has helped me.'"

Sam wouldn't have thought he could be even more astonished than he already was. "*I* helped him? Me? But he must have made a mistake! I never met him!"

"And yet you're here, aren't you? He also told me I would see you only after his death. He left this world exactly sixty-eight days ago. The funeral will take place the day after tomorrow."

"And . . . you're going to help me?"

The priest stood up and walked over to the largest chest. He opened it and took out an amphora and two clay goblets.

"I have some honey beer here. Would you like to taste it?"

Sam nodded and took a goblet. The beverage was both tart and sweet, and slightly prickly on the tongue. Not bad at all.

"When I was little," continued Ahmosis, sitting back down, "there was a room in the house that no one was allowed to enter. That's where my father kept the objects I mentioned, the ones from his travels. After a while, rumors began to spread, thanks to the servants, I suppose. People started to say Setni had magical objects of great power. If you ask me, those are the objects that interested my cousin the scribe. If I had died last night, he would have been able to claim them. Kamosis has always been hungry for glory." He drank a swallow of beer with an amused look. "Unfortunately for him, he would have been disappointed!"

"Do you mean those things don't exist?"

"That they no longer exist! My father destroyed nearly all of them before he died. He was well aware that the rumors would feed envy, and he didn't want his house or his death profaned by thievery. He wasn't wrong."

"But in that case," Sam said worriedly, "how will you be able to help me?"

"Setni gave me this for you."

Slowly Ahmosis took off one of the big rings gracing his right hand. It was a circle of gold topped by a round, amber-colored translucent disk inscribed with the image of a beetle. The beetle carried a perfect red pearl on its back.

"Do you know what the scarab represents for us? It means both 'being' and 'becoming.' You must have seen them skittering along the ground, rolling a ball of grass before them. The scarab is the one that moves as well as the one that carries. My father made me swear to keep this ring with me until his burial. He assured me that if you were indeed the boy he was thinking of, you would know what to do with it."

Just then someone knocked twice on the door.

"Ahmosis!" cried a muffled voice. "The vizier's envoy is here!"

The priest looked annoyed. "Forgive me, I'm going to have to leave you again. It won't take long."

He promptly went out, leaving Sam with the ring. The boy turned the amber scarab over and over in his palm. "The one that moves and the one that carries." Setni may have met Sam in one of the high priest's dreams, but he certainly hadn't provided a user's manual for scarabs.

Sam gulped down the rest of his goblet of beer. The beverage produced a pleasantly warm sensation that calmed his anxiety. *Note to self: Don't become an alcoholic*, he thought. Okay, now for this ring . . . The scarab was about three quarters of an inch in diameter, completely flat, its carapace and legs delicately carved into the glass. The red pearl made a perfectly round, smooth bump on top. What did Sam need to return to his world? A kind of coin or medal with a hole in the middle. Could he use this jewel in its present state on the stone statue, which was probably hidden somewhere in Setni's tomb? No. Conclusion? He had to separate the scarab from the pearl and the ring. If he forced it and smashed the beautiful ring left to Ahmosis by his father . . . that was a chance he had to take.

He tried to unscrew the ring from the scarab, and after some effort heard a kind of click. The pearl was attached to the ring through an opening in the insect's body, and the three elements came apart with no trouble. The glass scarab now had a beautiful hole in its center and would serve very well as a magic coin. His ticket home! Because he was going home!

Provided the walls and ceiling stopped swaying, that is . . .

"I'm terribly sorry," said Sam.

He had a horrible headache, as if he had spent twelve hours with his head jammed in a vise. The sun burned his eyes, and he could barely use his legs.

"It's my fault," Ahmosis reassured him. "I should never have given you that beer on an empty stomach."

They stood together in front of Setni's tomb. From this height, the Nile Valley panorama was impressive. The sun was at its zenith, and the little village of Set Maat lay sweltering in the heat. Sam thought of Peneb, Nout, Didou, and Biatou. They had become almost like family to him. He would have liked to see them again, but Ahmosis had very little time available: The vizier had requested his presence early in the afternoon. The investigation had moved forward rapidly, and Mekhnat and the scribe's guilt was no longer in doubt. But Ahmosis had wanted to accompany Sam this far.

"Are you thinking of the workers, Sem? Don't worry, I will speak to the vizier on their behalf. If necessary, I have some grain stored — enough to keep them until new supplies arrive."

"That's . . . that's very nice of you. I don't know how to thank you."

"I'm the one who owes you thanks, Sem. You have accomplished what my father would have wished for you. It is almost as if he were still among us."

He hugged Sam.

"I am going to let you continue alone. It wouldn't be good for me to know too much. That was Setni's desire."

Sam was torn between the emotion of the moment and the fear of setting off for another unknown world.

"Did he really not tell you anything else? I mean . . . I'm not sure I'm going to make it back home. I want to, really badly, but I don't know how to go about it."

Ahmosis looked at him in surprise. He thought for a moment, then said, "I know much less about it than you, Sem. Or perhaps . . . One time my father stayed away a very long time. Days and days. My mother even wondered if some misfortune had befallen him. When he finally returned, he looked thin and tired, but he was smiling. He kissed us all tenderly and said: 'One of you was thinking of me so hard that it guided me home.' He never said anything further, unfortunately." He placed his hand on Sam's shoulder. "May Amon-Re show you the way in turn."

Sam thanked him again, then took the torch Ahmosis had prepared and entered Setni's tomb. The darkness did his eyes good. He ran down the two flights of stairs, went along the marvelously decorated hallways, skirted the well, and reached the rope ladder. He dropped his torch down the hole and climbed down into the hall. It was even more beautiful than the other rooms, completely decorated in gold leaf, with many representations of the god Thoth. Luxurious chairs, stools, statuettes, baskets, and jars had now been installed to accompany the dead man on his final journey.

Sam examined the enormous block in the center of the room, where the sarcophagus would soon be set. A stone emblem had been carved into its base, with a sun and six very long rays pointing downward. It was the Egyptian version of the stone statue. Sam's breathing quickened; he wanted to get this over with as quickly as possible. He took off the ring, unscrewed the scarab, and found it almost warm. As he approached the carving, he said an improvised prayer:

"Please let someone be thinking about me! Please let someone be thinking about me!"

CHAPTER NINE

A Family Meeting

"Sam?"

Gradually the fire burning Sam's body eased. A few yards away, the shout rang out again:

"Sam?"

He recognized the cement dust under his fingers and the familiar smell of old paper. The basement . . . He was back! He had returned to his own time!

"Sammy!"

Both emotion and nausea overwhelmed him, and he crumpled to the ground, coughing and weeping. He felt a hand on his shoulder.

"Sammy!"

It was Lily's hand. Never in his wildest dreams could he have imagined he would be so happy to see his cousin again!

"Lily!" he blurted, still gagging. "You were the one who was thinking about me!"

"Sammy, how did you . . . ?"

Her eyes were wide with surprise and her mouth was making a funny sort of O.

"Sammy, how did you . . . ?"

Lily seemed to be doing everything twice.

"That's okay, Lily. I can hear you fine!"

She helped him up, then led him over to the bed, repeating each of her gestures each time: She reached her arm out to him, then took it back, then reached out again. It took Sam two full minutes to realize that he was experiencing an illusion: He was seeing each movement doubled, in a kind of echo, the way a shout in an empty room bounces back from the walls. His leaps through time must have altered his sense perception, which explained this feeling of repetition and déjà vu.

After he sat quietly for a moment, however, the effect began to wear off. A distraught Lily knelt by his feet, looking at him.

"Sammy, where were you? How did you get here? There was no one here. I was all alone!"

Sam rubbed his face to make sure he wasn't dreaming. But no: the basement, the cot, the little lamp . . . He suddenly noticed that he was still wearing a loincloth, while his blue jeans and T-shirt from *before* lay folded on the pillow.

He didn't understand anything except that he was happy to be home.

"What . . . what day is it?"

"Sunday," said Lily, looking at her watch. "Sunday, June 6, to be precise, at 5:12 p.m."

Sunday! Just one day after Saturday, while he had been gone for at least a week!

"Are you going to explain this to me, Sam? Everybody's been looking for you since last night! Grandma was going nuts. We even called the police. We thought that you'd run away, or . . . who knows what!"

"The police . . ." Sam muttered. "What about Dad?"

Lily hesitated. "No news," she said at last. "Well, you can rest here if you like, and I'll call Grandma. She'll come and pick us up and . . ."

"No, Lily, wait. Not Grandma. Not the police. Listen to me first."

And he began to tell her, in an irrepressible flood of words, about his adventures in time. How he found the stone statue behind the tapestry, how it led him to Iona, the monastery, the Vikings, running away; the ruined village of Fleury, the bombardments, Corporal Chartrel's medal; how he had found himself in Setni's tomb, the village of Set Maat, Ahmosis and the Million-Year Temple . . . Lily listened openmouthed, sometimes exclaiming with astonishment — "Hieroglyphics?" — or enthusiasm — "Too cool!" It reassured Sam somewhat that she didn't seem to think he was completely crazy.

"The Million-Year Temple, you said?" she asked when he was finished. "Have you read this?" She showed him the big red book with the thick cover he had noticed the day before. "There," she said, pointing.

The book was open to a chapter titled "Thebes, the Hundred-Gated City." An old-fashioned engraving showed the Temple of Ramses — Ramses III, as Sam now learned — the way it looked to a visitor at the beginning of the last century: in ruin, partly buried in the sand, its gigantic wall and columns in pieces after three thousand years of neglect.

"I was there," said Sam with a sigh. "I was there! Do you believe me?"

Lily stared at him. "I don't know where else you could have found that loincloth thing you're wearing!" she said with a flash of her old sarcasm. Then she softened: "All of your clothes were on the floor over there. I put them on the bed. And there was this coin . . ."

She held out a coin with a hole in it, covered with Arabic inscriptions. It was the coin that had made his first journey possible. "It was next to the stone statue, as you call it."

Sam nodded slowly, torn with contradictory emotions. "So you believe me?"

"Of course I believe you, Sam! I'm your cousin, aren't I? And besides, you haven't seen everything! Here!"

She quickly flipped the pages of the red book under his nose: 70, 72, 74, . . . every spread in the book was identical! The phrase "Thebes, the Hundred-Gated City" was repeated a hundred times, two hundred times! The same engraving of the Million-Year Temple, the same text about Ramses III. It was like a spectacular printing mistake!

"But it showed something different yesterday!" Sam cried. "When I opened it, it was about some guy named Vlad Tepes, this really bloody king from Vallikia or Wallachia or something. . . . I don't remember anymore."

"The *entire* book?"

"I don't know. I only looked at one page."

"So you can't say for sure that they all looked the same yesterday?"

"I didn't pay a lot of attention. I had just found the storage room." He had a sudden thought. "What about you? How do you happen to be here?"

Lily gave him a slightly superior look — which pretty much fit the Lily he knew — and casually brushed back her hair.

"Grandpa alerted the police this morning and had to come

to the bookstore with them. The keys were still in the door, and your bag was next to the stairs. They figured you'd run away or that you had gone to visit a friend. But I knew better, because you don't have a lot of friends, and if you'd wanted to run away, you wouldn't have abandoned your bag or left the bookstore open. And kidnappers would have taken more than just you: There are a ton of valuable old books here, and it doesn't look as if anything was stolen. So I told myself that one way or another, you were still in the house, and since your bag was on the way to the basement, I thought I should start here."

Sam couldn't keep from whistling in admiration.

"The thing is, my mother came back with her boyfriend last night and he insisted on spending the night at Grandma's. Supposedly Mr. I'm-Smarter-Than-Everybody-Else wants to 'support us in these difficult times.' As if we needed him!" she snapped. "I had no intention of watching him show off all day with Mom applauding. So I told them I was going to Jennifer's this afternoon, got your keys, and came to see for myself."

"You did that for me?" Sam was astonished.

"Well, let's not exaggerate," she shot back. "Mainly for Grandpa and Grandma! If you could see the mood at home! In fact, we better go there," she said, looking at her watch. "The police can come look at the stone statue tomorrow, and they'll figure it out!"

"No way!" Sam declared. "The police would take over everything — the room and the book — and they'll take the stone to a laboratory to analyze it. My father will never be able to come home."

"What?"

"Come on, Lily, don't you get it?" said Sam, his certainty

growing as he spoke. "My father set all this up. And that's where he's gone — back in God knows what time! If anyone happened to damage or remove the statue, he would be stuck centuries from now! That's why he hid it so carefully!"

"Do you think so?"

"Definitely! We can't talk about it to anyone!"

"Not even to Grandma or Grandpa?"

"It would just scare them more. Particularly since nobody can help him. I mean nobody here, in *our* time. We have to wait for him to come back and not touch the statue. It's a question of life or death, do you understand?"

Sam sounded so vehement that Lily backed away from him. Just then, a cheerful snatch of music rang out on the other side of the tapestry: the "Boy on the Beach" tune, which Lily used as a ringtone.

"That's for me!"

Lily ran to the door, and Sam followed her. From her pink bag she pulled a brand-new cell phone that was blinking like a Christmas tree. "Hello . . . yes, Mom. No, I'm still at Jennifer's. Yes, don't worry, I'm coming home . . . In twenty minutes? All right." She hung up.

"Nice ringtone," Sam teased.

Lily shrugged. "I don't care if you like it or not. Rudolf just brought me the phone from Singapore. It's got Internet, IM, a camera, an MP3 player . . . He thinks he can buy me off with stuff, but I still think he's a jerk."

"What about your mother?"

"She wants me to come home. What are we going to tell them?"

"That we just ran into each other in front of the house."

"But what about you?

"I'll make something up. It can't be worse than the Vikings, can it?" He hefted Lily's bag. "Do you think we could fit the book in here?"

It was incredible how good cheese rolls and peanuts could taste! And soda. Sam hadn't had a soda since forever! It was much better than beer!

"You look as if you haven't eaten all day," Grandma said, sniffling but smiling at the same time. She slid her arm around his shoulders. "We were so frightened!"

"You really could have warned us," chimed in Aunt Evelyn, her mouth pinched. "Do you realize how much worry you caused your grandparents?"

Sam kept his head bent and continued to down the crunchy cheesies and the delicious salted peanuts. The virtues of silence!

Also seated at the table were Grandpa, who was staring at the ceiling, and Rudolf, Lily's stepfather. "Stepfather" was actually an exaggeration, since he and Evelyn weren't married. They had been going out for a few years, at first very discreetly, then more openly for the last seven or eight months. Sam didn't much like his Aunt Evelyn. When the Faulkners lived in the big Bel View house, she would come by often to whine and complain. Sam remembered long, tiresome talks where she bemoaned how hard it was to raise a child alone and criticized her brother Allan for not understanding her situation.

Then Evelyn met Rudolf, and she changed: She cried less but yelled more. When Allan lost his wife, Evelyn offered "advice" at every turn: You shouldn't sell the Bel View house, you shouldn't buy a bookstore, you shouldn't wear black, you shouldn't change your son's school, you should sign him up for hockey instead of judo . . . It was nice to see her be more confident, but Sam and his father both wished she'd lay off every so often.

Apparently unable to bear Sam's silence, Aunt Evelyn continued the attack: "And what were you up to those two days you were missing?"

"I walked around," answered Sam.

"You walked around? Who do you think you're kidding? Your grandmother was worried sick, and you were walking around?"

"Don't be so hard on him," Grandma broke in. "You know that Sammy has been a little at sea lately. We haven't had news of Allan for ten days, and that's not easy for him."

"There you go," Evelyn said with a scowl. "If people had listened to me, we would have made Allan see a psychiatrist a long time ago. It isn't normal to live hidden away with all those dusty books and old memories." She gave a short, bitter laugh. "With a life like that, how can you expect Samuel *not* to have problems?"

The Samuel in question decided not to respond to that; he didn't care about Aunt Evelyn. The bag of peanuts, on the other hand . . .

"And where did you sleep?" Evelyn continued.

"At the train station," Sam lied.

"At the station? You could have been mugged!"

"There was a train at the platform and I slipped inside."

"What was the train like?" asked Rudolf in a detached tone.

Sam looked at him. Rudolf was about ten years older than

Evelyn. He had a perfect tan, graying temples, and a square jaw, and he often traveled overseas for his import-export business. He never missed a chance to give Lily the latest, most expensive toys, like the cell phone, but he never managed to win her over either; Lily still resented him for stealing her mother away. Sam wasn't sure of his own feelings about Rudolf, but he was bothered by the fact that the man didn't seem to believe his story.

"It was an ordinary train, with seats and windows," he answered.

"At the station, eh? I heard the city was having the platforms guarded. There was some vandalism last year. Weren't you afraid of the dogs?"

"Nah, I've always wanted to have one," Sam shot back. "More than I want a fake uncle, anyway," he added under his breath.

"Do you hear that insolence?" Evelyn said angrily to Sam's grandparents. "Do you hear how he speaks to Rudolf? This is what happens when you don't control your son!"

"Let it go, darling," said Rudolf magnanimously. "It isn't his fault. What Sam needs is more discipline, more authority. Has Allan thought about boarding school? I know an excellent one in the United States. They straighten kids out in just two years, and they toe the line after that, believe me."

Sam rose noisily from his chair. "Excuse me. I'm going to go to bed. Those train seats weren't very comfortable."

As he passed, Rudolf grabbed his wrist and looked at the marks on his arm. "A bit of a hothead, our Sammy, eh?" he remarked. "These scratches . . . did you get into a fight?"

Sam jerked his arm away. He would have loved to say that

he'd gotten scratched in the bushes at the Temple of Ramses, but he didn't think Rudolf would appreciate it. "There was a cat in the train car," he said.

Rudolf didn't take his gaze from Sam, who could see something hostile in his eyes. This guy wasn't a pretentious jerk; he was a dangerous jerk.

"You aren't doing drugs, are you, Sam?" he asked quietly. "Because that would explain a lot."

"It's nice of you to be interested, Rudolf. But I already have a father for that."

As he left, the silence in the room was electric. He had barely gotten to his bedroom upstairs when he heard Evelyn burst out: "Papa, did you see the nerve of him? And you don't say anything? He must be a terrible influence on Lily!"

"My poor Evelyn." Grandpa sighed impatiently. "You'll never understand anything about children."

Sam slammed the door to shut out the rest.

He was tempted to go to bed immediately, but instead he took out the new Hot Pickles album, put on his headphones, and sat down at his computer. Under other circumstances, he would have played some Counter-Strike online, but tonight he felt an urgent need to reconnect with the worlds he had left behind . . . to reassure himself that some sign of them remained, that they had once been real, that his adventures weren't just products of his imagination.

He typed "Thebes" into his search engine, then "Setni" and "Ahmosis." Photos popped up showing the modern city, the vestiges of the palace on the west bank of the Nile, the ruined workers' village and the ocher-colored cliff studded with tombs. Sam found himself choking up as he looked at the pictures of the workers' village, which had been abandoned three millennia ago: Peneb had lived there . . . and Nout. . . . He found nothing definite about Setni and Ahmosis, except for an old Egyptian legend: Tradition had it that one "Setni" was a sorcerer who stole the god Thoth's *Great Book of Magic*, setting off a series of tragedies. Was it the same Setni? It was tempting to think so.

Sam then typed in "Fort Souville" and "World War I," and found an extensive description of the 1916 Battle of Verdun. Fighting had raged in the area for months, causing hundreds of thousands of deaths; the village of Fleury had been wiped off the map. Sam shivered. In its way, the Internet was also a time machine.

But Sam had his greatest shock on the Web sites about Iona. After searching around a little for Colm Cille's story, he came across images of the island exactly the way he had known it, with its treeless moors, its low stone walls, its changing sky. And by clicking on a series of specialized links, he found extraordinary images of the Gospel that Ranald Tallman had shown him in the scriptorium — the same writing, the same figures, the same colors! The text that accompanied the reproductions said: "According to one theory, this manuscript, one of the most beautiful to have come down to us from the Middle Ages, was begun around the year 800 by the monks of the abbey of Iona. After a destructive attack by Vikings, it was miraculously saved and brought to Ireland, where other monks completed it."

Sam found himself laughing and crying at the same time. The miracle — that had been him!

CHAPTER TEN

Press Review

On his first day back at school, Sam was completely out of it. His problems began in first-period math, when he realized the homework he had postponed the week before was now due immediately. He had vaguely planned to get to it on Sunday, but it was hard to find a calculator in the places he'd spent the weekend.

Worse yet, Mrs. Cubert had a sixth sense for this sort of thing. First she gazed at the class as a group, her nose in the air like a dog on point, sniffing for the scent of undone homework. When she was sure of her facts, she pointed at Sam.

"Mr. Faulkner, please come show us how sustained effort is the foundation of all mathematical progress."

She was in the habit of coming up with obscure sayings like that, leaving you uncertain whether to stay glued to your chair or rush immediately to the blackboard. For Sam it was apparently the blackboard. He stood up without enthusiasm.

"Aren't you taking your papers, Faulkner? Is that courage or rashness?"

He grabbed a half-scribbled page from his notebook, while

his friend Harold muttered, "We'll send an ambulance for you, Sam. Don't worry, I'll tell your family!"

Given a visored helmet and a three-foot sword, Mrs. Cubert would have made an excellent Viking. What followed was possibly the least pleasant fifteen minutes of Sam's existence (made worse by the shower of spit that rained down from the vociferous Mrs. Cubert) as he battled a series of convoluted equations, chalk in hand. After mainly demonstrating the extent of his ignorance, Sam sat back down with a D and three extra exercises to do.

At recess, Harold took him aside: "So, did your dad come back?"

"No," said Sam, his jaw set. He was dying to tell Harold everything, but a little alarm went off in his brain: *If you do that, and if Harold doesn't believe you, you'll be made fun of through the end of the year at least. Is that what you want?* Once again, restrained and tense, he fell back on the virtues of silence.

Anyway, Harold had already started another subject. "Hey, you didn't come to Maddy's party on Saturday."

"Er, no, I didn't."

"She asked me if you were sick."

"Ah."

Maddy was a girl in the class who had been circling him since the start of the year. Sam thought she was attractive and nice, but — how could he put it? — he just wasn't interested. And the reason he wasn't interested was named Alicia Todds.

Thinking about Alicia now, Sam felt a familiar ache. Alicia Todds had been his best friend when he lived in the Bel View neighborhood, up until the time they were ten or eleven. She was a delicate beauty with long blond hair; big blue eyes; soft, pale skin; an angelic smile . . . and she was, without a doubt, the most wicked prankster Sam had ever met. After grouchy Mr. Roger yelled at Sam for accidentally skateboarding into his garbage cans, a pizza truck showed up at the old man's door with seven anchovy-bacon pizzas, seven double-cheese chorizos, and seven two-liter bottles of soda, none of which he had ordered. Alicia caught his reaction on film with her camera, but she paid the price when her parents discovered the photo and forced her to apologize to the pizzeria. But even then she managed to get the pizzeria manager to buy her an ice-cream cone, because no one resisted Alicia Todds's charm. The Todds lived next door to the Faulkners, so she and Sam hung out every afternoon, and their families occasionally vacationed together at the Todds's house by the shore.

But when Sam's mother died, everything changed; Sam sometimes felt almost as if he had died himself. He had stopped feeling anything, wanting anything, communicating with anyone, even his father; and in this state of complete disconnection, he stopped talking to Alicia altogether. Once she burst into tears at his coldness, and the last time she came to visit (he could hardly bear to think about it), he had shut the door in her face. It was as if all the good times were past, and any new pleasure would be an insult to his mother's memory. So no more walking home from school together, no more daylong video game sessions, no more pillow fights on Saturday night, no more trips to the seaside. In the months that followed, the Faulkners moved, Sam changed schools, and Alicia went out of his life.

But not out of his heart.

When he finally took an interest in life again, he missed

her more than anyone else. He so often wanted to go back to Bel View! To knock on her door, to tell her how guilty he felt, that he was sorry he had caused her pain. But he had never dared, and now nearly three years had gone by. From time to time Sam spotted Alicia downtown — she had become a very pretty girl, slim and tall, with an elegant, catlike walk — and every time it was like a stab in the heart. Two or three times, Sam had dialed the Todds's phone number, but he hadn't had the courage to let it ring. If Alicia ever thought of him, she must hate him. And she was surely so different now!

"Sam, are you listening to me?" Harold said.

"Huh?"

"You weren't paying attention. I was telling you that Simon's going out with Maddy now."

"Oh."

The recess bell spared Sam from having to explain to Harold why his mind was elsewhere. But Mr. Maverick, the science teacher, quickly brought him back to earth. He handed out the final grades of the year, and Sam received only a C–. Would this threaten his chances of moving up to the next grade? In the ten days since his father disappeared, Sam hadn't done much work in any of his classes, and his unimpressive marks reflected that. And with school coming to an end, there was no way to make them up.

From the corner of his eye he watched Maddy and Simon, who were two rows away, discreetly holding hands under the table. Maddy and Simon . . . the Saturday party . . . For some incomprehensible reason, Sam felt a wave of jealousy. Why couldn't something go right for *him*?

Without thinking, he raised his hand.

"Excuse me, sir. Can I ask you a question? It isn't really directly connected to the class, but . . ."

Mr. Maverick looked at his watch to see how much time he could give Sam without slowing down the lesson. "Ask away, Faulkner."

"Is it possible to go back in time?"

All the students looked at Sam in amazement. Even Maddy let go of Simon's hand.

"Well, Faulkner, that's an interesting question — and you're right, it has nothing to do with today's lesson." The teacher looked at him, his eyes narrowed maliciously. "Would you like to go back a week and redo your science homework? It seems to me you could have gone over it a few more times."

There were several laughs.

"To make this short, let's say that in theory going back in time is not impossible, at least for light particles. Imagine that you're on Earth and your friend Harold is on Mars. If you send him a fairly powerful light signal at 11 a.m., it will take about twenty-five minutes for this signal to reach Mars. So at 11:05, you can think of the signal as having been in your past for five minutes, but it's still part of your neighbor's future: He will have to wait twenty more minutes to receive it. Which incidentally shows us that time is a relative notion; the present, past, and future aren't the same for each one of us, but depend on what we are and where we are. Very well.

"Now, Faulkner, let's suppose you have a rocket that can go twice as fast as your light signal. If you take off from Earth at 11:05, you have a good chance of catching up with your signal at around 11:10. In other words, at 11:10, *you will have caught up with your past!* And in a certain way you will have gone back in time. In any case, that's the principle. Now you would need to build a rocket that could go faster than the light signal — that is, faster than the speed of light itself, which as you know is the fastest known speed in the universe. So as a practical matter, the experiment is impossible. In other words, Faulkner, unless you are able to go back in time a week, you will have to be satisfied with your grade!"

Sam nodded, even though he hadn't grasped all the details. He didn't tell Maverick that he had the rocket in the basement of Faulkner's Antique Books — and it looked like a prehistoric peanut dispenser!

After lunch, Sam was able to enjoy a two-hour respite, thanks to Miss Delaunay's art class. At last, a subject where he felt comfortable, which gave him a feeling of real accomplishment. Drawing a tree on a canvas, feeling the leaves tremble under his charcoal, seeing the bark thicken under his brush, one stroke at a time, as the soft, glistening colors suddenly gave it life — it filled him with a happiness he hadn't known since his father disappeared.

"Not bad, Sam," said Miss Delaunay appreciatively. "Add a drop of turpentine — your paint will be easier to work with, and brighter too. But you're gifted!"

That was his only compliment of the day. English class was just a long series of boring remarks about a really stupid poem; Sam prayed for the class to be over as quickly as possible — for the guy in the poem to go bowling or something instead of weeping over his girlfriend for verse after verse. When the bell finally rang, he grabbed his skateboard and rushed for the exit. He needed air, oxygen! No more walls, no more windows! No more Simon, no more Maddy! He raced along the sidewalk toward the bus stop without paying any attention to the few friends who greeted him. He needed to be alone.

When he reached the main intersection, however, he broke out in a cold sweat. Monk and two of his stooges were leaning against the bus stop sign. Sam would have turned around, but Monk was already on him.

"Faulkner!" he barked, jumping up with surprising speed. "You little punk!" His hand, which was twice the size of Sam's, closed on him like a clamp. "I've been waiting for you!"

"Waiting for me?" stammered Sam.

"Do you have my twenty bucks?"

"Your what?"

"My twenty bucks, to pay me for the computer circuits you ruined the other day?"

"Ah, no, but I . . ."

From the corner of his eye, Sam watched Monk's enormous hand, which had suddenly closed into a fist and was showing clear signs of impatience. His two buddies looked on with glee, waiting for the moment when the mass of bone and flesh would flatten Sam's nose.

"Well then, like I promised, I'm going to pay myself back with your teeth."

"Monk!" Sam tried. "You . . . you're not going to do that, are you? What about Saturday's competition? If Master Yaku learns that you beat me up outside the gym . . ."

"And you're the one who's going to tell him?" said Monk, still more threatening.

"No, but say I wasn't able to go, and that I had to forfeit because of . . . uh, you know. He'll ask for an explanation and . . . you know what Sensei is always saying? 'Never violence, always self-mastery! Save your energy for the mats!'"

Sam wasn't sure that this would work, but he didn't have anything else handy. Besides, Monk had always displayed boundless admiration for Yaku.

"For the mats, eh?" Monk said, hesitating slightly. His powerful fist suddenly relaxed and a cunning light came into his eyes. "Okay, shrimp. We'll meet on Saturday at the tournament, where I'll flatten you in front of *everybody*. And you better be there, or else . . ." He made a gesture that meant that he would snap Sam in half like a Popsicle stick.

"Of course I'll be there!" answered Sam in a falsely cheerful tone. "I wouldn't miss it for the world!"

Monk straightened Sam's T-shirt with suspicious care, as if he wanted to keep his victim whole until the day of the sacrifice.

"Okay, see you Saturday, Faulkner. And don't try to trick me."

"Of course not, Monk!"

Deep down, Sam mentally booked a ticket to the North Pole for Saturday.

"Is something the matter, Sam? You're all pale."

Grandpa had come to sit across from Sam in the kitchen as the boy ate his second cookie without enthusiasm.

"I'm okay."

"You're worried about your father, aren't you? That's normal, but I don't think you should get too worked up about it. He's disappeared before."

"For two or three days," Sam objected. "Never for twelve."

"I'm not talking about lately. I mean before this, before you were born."

Sam swallowed his last mouthful of cookie. "You mean this happened before I was born too?"

"Yes, about twenty years ago, when Allan was studying history in college. One summer he left for three months to do an internship in Egypt with a well-known archeologist — Professor Chamblin or Chamberlain, I can't remember."

Grandpa tried to smile, as if he were telling an ordinary story, but Sam could sense there was something else behind it. A dig in Egypt — that couldn't just be a coincidence.

"You know that your father has always been a collector, right? He has a whole binder upstairs on the dig. I even cut out a few of the articles myself."

"Upstairs? In the attic?"

"Yes. Your grandmother must have put that in one of her trunks. She never throws anything away either!"

"And what happened, exactly?"

"I can't really say. During the dig they made some discoveries: tombs, sacred objects . . . you can read the articles if you're interested. But that's not the main thing. The main thing is that at the beginning, your father phoned us every day. And then suddenly, nothing! For three days in a row! You can imagine how worried your grandmother was. After a lot of difficulty, I managed to get the phone number at the camp, and they told me that Allan had disappeared. The team was convinced that he had found the dig too hard and gone home, along with another intern his age. And we might have agreed, except Allan hadn't warned us!"

As he often did, Grandpa was looking up at the ceiling, speaking as much to himself as to Sam.

"That lasted two whole weeks, two terrible weeks. And

then one morning, he phoned. His explanations weren't very clear. He said that he'd wanted to travel in the desert, and it wasn't always easy to call us, but now he'd rejoined the dig for the rest of his internship and he'd call us every day. And then, five or six days later, the same thing happened again — no news! It was like that for two months. One week he'd be at the dig, another he'd disappear, the next one he'd come back, and so on. Your grandmother and I nearly went over there, but that wasn't easy with the grocery store. Finally he came home in October."

Sam could easily imagine what kind of "trips" his father had been taking.

"Did you find out what happened?"

Grandpa lowered his gaze to Sam. "Well, actually we didn't. He was in no shape to tell us. He had caught some rare virus, and he lost twenty pounds and a few handfuls of hair. He spent a month in a clinic that specialized in exotic illnesses."

Ancient illnesses, Sam corrected him mentally. "And these disappearances, were there any more after that?"

"Not that I know of. Or else just little ones. Two years later he met your mother and settled down a lot. A little later they got married, and then you came along."

"Dad never told me about this," said Sam, forcing himself to finish his glass of orange juice as calmly as possible. "Can I take a look at that binder?"

"If you don't get lost in all that junk! I have to go pick up your grandmother from her bridge club. We can talk more about this later, if you like."

Sam didn't need to be told twice. He raced up to the attic to explore the trunks and the jumble Grandma faithfully stored there. There was out-of-date furniture and old clothes, including lots of jackets embroidered with FAULKNER'S GROCERY, from the time his grandparents lived in the United States. A black-and-white photo album showed a picture of Grandpa's father standing outside their Chicago store. He shoved aside Allan's wooden toys, schoolbooks, children's clothes, and the famous collection of fingernail clippings, and finally spied a binder labeled EGYPT in black marker.

Sam sat down under the skylight and began reading. There were about twenty articles in all, yellowed and more or less neatly cut out, stored in transparent sleeves in chronological order. At first glance they seemed to be excerpts from several specialized magazines and an English-language Egyptian newspaper, *The Cairo Times*.

ARCHEOLOGIA, APRIL 1985:
Archeology Internship in Egypt

Professor Chamberlain is planning a new dig from June to November 1985, near the Valley of the Kings at Thebes. His goal is to uncover new tombs of the 20th Dynasty. If you are a student in history, art history, or archeology, and you are available this summer, Prof. Chamberlain would like you to consider joining his team and participating in an archeological adventure of the greatest importance. (Food and lodging are provided, but not transportation.) Send your transcripts and a letter explaining your interests to: 7 Lower Street, Cambridge, England. Tel: (01223) 2589734.

With this announcement, everything had begun.

THE CAIRO TIMES, 21 JUNE 1985:

Professor Chamberlain's Hopes

The eminent English archeologist, who is currently on an important dig in the Thebes region, says that he is confident of discovering some unknown tombs from the 20th Dynasty. "The hills above the temples of Ramses III and Queen Hatshepsut have not yet given up all of their secrets," he told our correspondent last night.

"Up to now we have mainly focused on the Valley of the Kings and the tombs of the pharaohs. Personally, I feel that the sepulchers of other great personalities, as well as those of the common people, have at least as much to teach us about the life and customs of the time."

Sam skipped over five or six articles that expanded on the same theme and stopped at this one:

THE CAIRO TIMES, 20 AUGUST 1985:

A Priest's Tomb Discovered at Thebes

From our special correspondent

Yesterday at 5 p.m., Professor Chamberlain and his team penetrated a richly decorated tomb that belonged to a priest of Amon of the 20th Dynasty (about 1180 B.C.). After a month of excavation on a site in Thebes West, they have opened a passage leading to the main hallway of the sepulcher. "It is splendid," said the English archeologist, who has decided not to rush the exploration of the tomb. "In order to avoid inflicting damage on the site, we are giving ourselves two weeks to reach the funerary chamber. Judging from the state of the first two rooms, I have reason to hope that the whole of the sepulcher is intact and the tomb has been spared by grave robbers." If that is the case, we hope Professor Chamberlain discovers as many marvels as Howard Carter did when he opened the tomb of Tutankhamen!

Over the next two weeks, several newspapers repeated the fact of the discovery, but once again *The Cairo Times* gave the most details:

THE CAIRO TIMES, 14 AUGUST 1985:
Exclusive! The Mysteries of Setni the Priest!

As we have written in earlier editions, Professor Chamberlain and his collaborators have finally reached the funerary chamber of the great priest Setni. After a great deal of work on the inscriptions that establish the identity of the tomb's owner, it would appear that . . .

Sam eagerly read the description of the funerary chamber, which sounded almost exactly as it was when he'd visited it by torchlight a few days earlier. Everything was still there, except that an enormous gold sarcophagus had been placed in the middle of the room. No mention was made of the sun design on the sarcophagus's pedestal, but the reporter did wonder about the nature of certain objects that accompanied the dead man:

But perhaps the most incredible objects in the room were a dozen coins from different eras: Roman sestertii,

Greek talents, medieval livres tournois — coins minted and circulated many centuries after Setni's burial! Asked about this mystery, Professor Chamberlain suggested that earlier visitors may have left the coins without stealing anything, homage to the memory of the great priest of Amon. This theory is far from attracting unanimous support, however, even among the professor's entourage.

The *Cairo Times* series stopped there, as if Allan Faulkner had been unable to collect any more articles. Was that the date he had started his "travels"? The following articles, which were all taken from scientific publications, provided little additional information — except perhaps for a final paragraph in the journal *Archeologia:*

ARCHEOLOGIA, OCTOBER 1985:
Rumors from the Work Site

The disappearance of several objects from the tomb of Setni the priest (20th Dynasty, 1180 B.C.) has occasioned endless rumors and discussion at Professor Chamberlain's work site at Thebes. Included among these objects are the famous coins supposedly dated from the Greek, Roman, and medieval eras, and therefore later than the sepulcher itself. Several scholars suggest a hoax was involved, and that the hoaxer retrieved the coins he himself had introduced, rather than be unmasked by Egyptian authorities. Whatever the case, the dig site is now under police supervision.

The binder ended there.

Had his father taken the coins to make the stone statue function? That was clearly the most likely explanation. But Grandpa had also spoken of another intern, who had disappeared at the same time Allan did, and under the same circumstances. Had both of them been using the stone? Or had the other intern stolen the coins? Sam couldn't wait to tell Lily about his discoveries.

CHAPTER ELEVEN

A New Departure

Sam had to wait three days for a chance to have a real talk with his cousin. During that time, Aunt Evelyn seemed to take Lily everywhere — the movies, swimming, shopping — probably hoping her daughter would forgive her for being away so much. Finally on Thursday, long after school was over, Lily came into Sam's bedroom with her book bag on her shoulder.

"I'm sorry, Sam, I didn't think my mother would ever let me go! I just have forty-five minutes before dance class. How are you doing?"

Sam stood up to close the door behind her, and showed her the binder, which he had hidden in a corner of his closet with the big red book. Quickly he explained the contents of the articles and the conclusions he had drawn from them about his father, the mysterious other intern, and the stone sculpture.

Lily frowned. "This Professor Chamberlain, did you try to find out who he was?"

"I found some information on the Internet. Chamberlain was a fairly well-known archeologist in the '70s and '80s, but the stuff in Thebes really hurt him. Some other archeologists suspected him of putting the coins in Setni's tomb himself to get attention, and people mentioned him less often after that. He died of cancer in 1995."

"What about the address in the article announcing the internship?"

"I called the number, but it's not in service anymore."

"Too bad," said Lily. "Someone might have given us a list of the people who went on the expedition and . . ."

She was interrupted by the grotesque "Boy on the Beach" ringtone.

"Mom? Yes, I'm at home . . . I'm getting ready. At five-thirty. No, no, I won't be late. . . . This evening? Okay, I'll make it. Okay, bye." She hung up, looking annoyed. "I'm not a kid anymore! Besides, how does she think I get along when she isn't around?"

"What's up?"

"Rudolf has two tickets for the opera this evening. He's taking Mom out to dinner right before the show starts and she won't be able to take me to dance class."

"I'll take you, if you like."

"To dance class?" she said, flattered. "Well, why not? Except I brought you something from the library and you may want to read it instead."

"What is it?"

"Not now. Let's finish the articles first. So you think your father first used the statue in Thebes?"

"You have any other ideas?"

"And then he stopped 'traveling,' as you call it, for a whole twenty years?"

"Hey, the statue was deep inside a tomb in Egypt! And guarded day and night, for sure."

"But then he found another statue — the one at the bookstore. In fact, that's probably why he moved to that weird neighborhood: Either the statue was already there or the house gave him the freedom to use it."

"That's what I think too," said Sam approvingly, impressed by his cousin's logical mind.

"Which would mean that he started traveling again two years ago, when he opened the bookstore," she continued. "Did you ever wonder why?"

Naturally, Sam had asked himself that question — and the answer wasn't especially pleasant. "If he was the one who stole the coins from Setni's tomb," he said reluctantly, "then anything's possible. He might use the stone statue to bring back old manuscripts, for example, or rare and valuable books."

The admission pained him, but he felt strongly that only the truth would help him bring his father back.

"Yes . . . though I don't really see your father as a book thief. But okay, for now let's suppose he uses the statue to get valuable books. How can he choose where he ends up in time? Because he can't just set out to go anywhere! And then how does he bring the books back with him?"

"He must know something we don't about how the statue works. Maybe there's a way to pick the time where you want to go?"

Lily sighed and looked at her watch. "Well, let's leave that for later. About the red book," she said with some intensity. "Have you thought about what I asked you the other day?

Whether all the pages were identical when you opened it the first time?"

"Like I said, I didn't pay much attention. But I remembered something else. On Iona, in the cave where the monks hid their books, there was this little book held together by a ring. It had twenty pages with the exact same image — a little drawing of an island that might have been Iona. And in Setni's tomb, I saw a bunch of papyri that had the same symbols on each sheet."

"What about the World War I time?" asked Lily.

"I didn't notice anything there. But it was too fast and everything was destroyed around me and . . ."

Lily sat down beside him and set the big book on her knees. "Want me to tell you what I think, Sammy?" Her eyes were shining.

"Go ahead."

"I think this book shows where a time traveler is in time. When I found it in the basement, it was all about Thebes and Ramses III, because that's where you were. If I'd looked at it a few hours earlier, it would have shown me the Iona monastery or World War I."

Sam was struck by the cleverness of her deduction. Of course! The red book was a kind of time compass, set to the period when the "traveler" landed! A Book of Time!

"But in that case, my father . . ." he began.

Lily pulled a small brochure with a scowling face printed on its cover from her bag. "The name you gave me Sunday," she continued, "the one you read in the book, that was Vlad Tepes, right?"

Sam nodded and took the little pamphlet. The title above

the picture was *Vlad Tepes or Dracula?: Between Myth and Reality*.

"Is this a joke?" he whispered.

"I looked it over, and Vlad Tepes was no joke. He was the guy who inspired the Dracula story. He lived in the fifteenth century in what's now Romania, in Eastern Europe."

Sam opened the brochure to the first page: "Vlad Tepes, also known as Vlad the Impaler or Dracula, prince of Wallachia, 1428?–1476." A biography of Vlad Tepes followed, illustrated with reproductions of old engravings.

"According to what's written there," continued Lily, "he wasn't actually a vampire. But he loved torturing people and killing his enemies, which is why he has that reputation."

Sam shuddered slightly. "When I opened the red book," he murmured, "it said 'Crimes and Punishments During the Reign of Vlad Tepes.' Do you . . . do you think my father went there?"

Lily didn't answer immediately, but her silence spoke volumes.

"The problem," she said, "is that since you've come back, nothing has changed in the Book of Time."

"What do you mean?"

"I mean that if your father had changed times, the book would have changed too, wouldn't it? All the pages would show whatever time he was in now. But instead it still shows Thebes, where you were."

"So you think he's stuck there?" Sam's voice was hollow.

"Well, it's not impossible, is it? Do you remember what was on the page, except for the title?"

"Not really," Sam admitted, making an effort to remember.

"I didn't know it was so important! It talked about torture and crimes, but . . ."

"Was there an illustration?"

"Yes — a castle, I think. Yeah, a castle, with a road running behind it."

"Then that's where your father is," Lily said grimly.

"He's a prisoner of Vlad Tepes?"

"Unless we've been wrong from the beginning . . ."

Sam felt tears of rage rise to his eyes and he threw the brochure violently onto his pillow. "Then we're wrong for sure! There's no way Dracula has my father in prison! Maybe the Book of Time doesn't work here. Maybe we have to leave it there next to the statue!"

Just then Sam noticed his cousin's cell phone on the bed. His anger left him instantly.

"Max! Max might know!"

"Max?"

"This guy who lives near the bookstore. My father phoned him before he disappeared. Maybe he told Max what he was planning to do or left a clue or something. Let's go talk to him. We can swing by the basement too, in case the Book of Time changes while we're seeing Max." Sam stood up and grabbed Lily's arm. "Come on!"

"But what about my dance class?"

"I need you, Lily. This is about my father."

She looked thoughtful, then stood up.

Barenboim Street was as lively as usual: Not a car, not a passerby, not even a cat disturbed the quiet street. Sam pressed

Max's doorbell for the third time, lengthily. "Mr. Max! Mr. Maaax!"

"Maybe he's not at home," suggested Lily.

"Are you kidding? He's as deaf as a rock. MR. MAAAX!"

The door finally opened to reveal a man in a worn bathrobe, his mustache rumpled and his eyes full of sleep. "Samuel Faulkner, as I live and breathe! And who is this young girl?

"She's my cousin Lily, Mr. Max."

"You say she's silly? But she looks so serious!"

"No, not silly," corrected Sam. "My cousin Lily, I said."

"A filly? Well, I suppose so, if that's an expression you boys use nowadays. And what's her name?"

"LILY!" she screamed, red as a peony.

"Lily! That's a great name, Lily! But there's no need to shout, I'm not deaf! Would you like something to drink?"

They followed Max into the kitchen, where nothing had changed for at least forty years: a Formica table and chairs, a white refrigerator with rounded corners, and a sink with copper faucets and chipped enamel. A set of plates — a gift from a gas station — hung on the wall, and a row of yellowed plastic vegetables lined the shelves.

"Would you like some Freshh!?"

This was the tricky moment in the visit. At some point in time, probably twenty years earlier, Max must have bought several cases of Freshh!, a brand of flavored lemonade that had mercifully disappeared from store shelves. He was almost certainly the only person in the world to have any bottles left, and he stubbornly insisted on serving it to his guests. The problem was that he didn't drink it himself. "I think I'd better have some whiskey instead," he would usually say apologetically. "Carbonated drinks don't sit well with me." Except that his Freshh! hadn't had a single bubble since 1987. And since no one ever visited him except for Sam . . .

Max took three glasses from the cabinet and set them on the table. "I think I'm going to have a whiskey instead," he thought aloud. "Carbonated drinks and I . . ." He poured them a generous glass of a yellowish liquid with a few sugar crystals floating in it, then served himself a stiff shot of liquor. Sam gestured to Lily that she should pretend to be drinking.

"By the way, Sam, the bookstore has been closed for a while now, hasn't it? Hasn't your father come back from his break?"

"Well, as a matter of fact, Mr. Max, that's what we want to talk to you about. We haven't had any news from him for thirteen days."

"No shoes for thirteen days? That must not be very practical, my boy, but I don't see the connection with your father!"

"HE DISAPPEARED THIRTEEN DAYS AGO," Sam shouted. "THAT'S WHY WE CAME TO SEE YOU!"

"Take it easy, boy! No point in getting worked up! I know perfectly well that I'm a little hard of hearing these days, but . . . wait a minute."

He got up and walked to the other side of the living room. Sam took advantage of this to hurriedly dump the two glasses into the sink. The drain made a strange, loud gurgle, as if the pipes were rebelling.

"It's disgusting," whispered Lily.

"But it unclogs you!"

Max returned with a small wooden box with SOUVENIR OF ARCADIA carved on top.

"I brought this back from Rustico," he said tenderly. "My brother and I spent a week there in 1947. The nicest vacation of my life."

From the box he took a copper horn that looked like the end of a trumpet, and stuck it in his ear. "Go ahead, my boy. This should work better now."

"My father left about two weeks ago. I know he telephoned you right before he left. I wondered if he told you where he was going."

"As I live and breathe!" exclaimed Max. "Two weeks ago? He certainly did visit me! That was the day that he told me about his vacation, in fact! He was hoping to do business down in the United States or some such."

Lily and her cousin exchanged a knowing glance.

"'And Sam,' I said, 'is he going with you?' — 'No,' he answered, 'he still has school. But I've prepared a surprise for him. If he ever comes to see you, give him this for me. He may find it useful while he's waiting for me to come back.'"

Max reached into the box, which was lined with a blue, white, and red flag with a yellow star. He took out a small cloth bag and held it out to Sam.

"'But only if he comes to see you, Max,' he insisted. 'If Sam just calls to chat, don't bother.'"

Clumsily, Sam undid the leather thong that held the sack closed, then turned it over onto his palm. A coin and a token fell out, both with holes in their centers.

"Bingo!" Sam said.

The token was made of shiny blue plastic, like a poker chip. The coin, on the other hand, was old and worn, almost black from use, with a wavy snake engraved on its face. He handed everything to Lily.

"Did he tell you anything else?"

"To be honest, no," said Max, scratching the few remaining hairs on his head. "Nothing important, anyway. What are those things?"

"Er, they're for a collection I've started. And did he seem . . . normal to you, that day?"

"Normal? Your father's never been a completely normal guy, Sam. That's why I like him so much! But no, he looked the way he usually does, maybe a little tired, no more. So he hasn't come back? Have you called the police?"

"The police have been told, yes."

"So he's disappeared," said Max, suddenly looking serious. "It's that house, I tell you. I knew it wasn't a great idea."

"That house? *Our house?* Why wasn't it a good idea, Max?"

"Your father didn't want me to tell you. Nor your grandmother, either — she's a good woman. But when your father wanted to move here, I advised him against buying that house. That house is why this neighborhood has a bad reputation! Why all the businesses have closed up shop! Why there's nobody left but us old people . . . That house, the Barenboim house! Not a lot of people would live there, believe me!"

"The 'Barenboim house'?" exclaimed Sam in surprise. "Like the name of the street? Who was this Barenboim guy?"

"A strange man, more than a hundred years ago. He lived there with a whole bunch of weirdos who went in and out at all hours of the day and night. Some would come, some would leave, never the same ones, all of them dressed any which way . . . a real circus! The Barenboim Gang, they were called. They weren't really nasty, but the neighborhood found them worrisome. Apparently there were fights too, and old man Barenboim wasn't shy about throwing a punch, they say. In any case, they wound up naming the street after him."

"Do you know anything else about him?"

"Not a thing," said Max, finishing his glass. "It's been ages! But now they say that house has the evil eye."

"Who lived there before my father?"

"This crazy woman, Martha Calloway. She never came out and always had a rifle at hand. Even the mailman didn't ring her bell. When she died, two years ago, it stank to high heaven! There were at least fifteen dogs in there! Your father was pretty brave to open a bookstore in a place like that."

Allan Faulkner, of course, had never informed his family of any of these minor "details." And for a very good reason: He wanted that house at all costs, because it contained the stone statue!

Sam stood up. "Thank you, Max. I really wanted these two coins for my collection! If I hear any news of Dad, I'll let you know."

He and Lily politely refused a second glass of Freshh! and went back to Faulkner's Antique Books.

Inside, there was still no sign that Allan had returned. Sam tried to play Lily the threatening message he'd heard on the answering machine — "All right, I've warned you" — but the recording had been erased.

"Grandpa must have rewound the cassette," Lily guessed, "in case your father showed up."

"Too bad," Sam said with a sigh. "But maybe it didn't mean anything. Take the Book of Time. I'll be downstairs in two secs."

While Lily went to the basement, he went up to his father's bedroom. He remembered the pile of white linen shirts and pants in his father's closet and was pretty sure now that he knew what they were for. When he slipped behind the unicorn tapestry five minutes later, Lily gave a cry of surprise:

"What are those pajamas? Are you going to bed?"

Sam modeled his new linen shirt and drawstring pants. "They aren't pajamas, they're my father's clothes. All natural fiber, to travel better."

"I don't understand."

"I'm just guessing here, but I don't think you can time-travel with modern fabrics. Anything artificial, synthetic, whatever. That's why my jeans and T-shirt stayed behind and the statue gave me that long shirt. You need clothing that is adapted to the period. My father must have had these clothes made up ahead of time. They're a little big for me, but if I roll up the sleeves . . ."

Lily couldn't believe her ears. "Sammy! You don't mean that you're going to leave again?"

"I have to, Lily. *He's a prisoner of Dracula!* And he's been there God knows how long! If I don't hurry, anything could happen. It might already be too late!"

"But how are you going to get there? Who's to say you'll land at the right spot and at the right time?"

"The coin," said Sam, trying to sound more confident than he really was. "Dad gave it to Max so that I could find it if something happened to him." He held up the metal disk with the snake. "I'm sure it's from the time of Vlad Tepes, and it'll take me right to his castle. Wasn't that what you figured out earlier?"

"I guess so," Lily said reluctantly. "But once you're there, you won't have a chance! That guy is completely crazy!"

"I'll be all right. I escaped from the Vikings, didn't I? And I survived a plot in the Temple of Ramses. . . ."

"But what about coming home?"

"That's where I need you, Lily. You have to think about me as often as possible. I know it sounds weird, but that's how Setni found his way home, and I think *your* thinking of me brought me back the other day. All you have to do is keep the book with you and . . . Hey, is there anything new in it?"

Lily was holding the big red book open on her lap. She turned it toward Sam: "Thebes, the Hundred-Gated City." Nothing had changed.

"That proves he's stuck there," said Sam. "With *Dracula*. I can't abandon him."

He gripped the coin in his fist and strode firmly to the stone sculpture. He was afraid he would lose his courage if he didn't go immediately.

"What about me?" Lily asked in a panicky voice. "What am I going to say?"

"Nothing. You don't know anything. If people ask you questions, just play dumb. Here, give me some light with that flashlight, would you?"

"But what about Grandpa and Grandma?"

"There's no other way, Lily. If I tried to explain it to them, they'd stop me from going. Or worse, they'd tell the police. And nobody can know."

He knelt in front of the stone statue as Lily came closer.

"Is that a sun?" she asked, shining the flashlight beam on the circle and the slits.

"Yeah, I think it's connected with the Egyptian religion or something."

"And that hole down below? What do you put in there? Maybe you can take things along, or —"

"I don't know," whispered Sam. "Don't come too close."

The metal disk was growing warmer in his hand, and his cousin's voice seemed to be coming from farther away. He gently set the coin in the center of the sun.

"Sam? Sammy, can you hear me?" said Lily, sounding as if she were on the other side of a wall. "We should try to —"

Sam put his hand on the rounded stone, and the ferocious heat exploded up his arm.

CHAPTER TWELVE

The Image-Makers' Guild

Sam slowly raised his head, trying not to gag. The walls of the basement had disappeared. He was in a cemetery, kneeling at the foot of a gray tombstone covered with a thick layer of snow. There was no inscription to be seen on the stone, but the rounded base of the cross bore the familiar signs: the sun, the slits, the opening under the . . .

"Lily," he murmured, wiping his mouth. "She was right!"

His cousin's cell phone lay in the center of the cavity. She must have put it there just before he touched the stone. Sam picked it up cautiously. Its screen read THURSDAY, JUNE 10, 5:42 P.M. — the time Sam had left. But what was the time and date *here*? Judging from the gray sky, snow, and icy wind, it was obviously winter. Sam was tempted to dial a number, but the icon indicated there was no network signal. The important thing was that Lily had guessed correctly: The cavity indeed served to transport objects! And his father must have used it to bring his books back!

Sam got to his feet. The cemetery looked deserted. It wasn't very big, maybe a hundred graves at most, bounded by a low wall and a small chapel. Beyond the whitened trees he could see some gently rolling hills that looked like scoops of melting vanilla ice cream. But there was no sign of Vlad Tepes's castle. Had the snake coin brought him to the wrong place?

Shivering, Sam headed for the chapel. Along the way, he scraped snow from a couple of tombstones: GUSTAV VEKEN, 1389–1427; PETRUS VAN HOOT, 1368–1411; MARGA WAAGEN, 1359–1429, etc. They were foreign names — though that didn't really mean anything — but he couldn't say if they sounded "Wallachian" or not. The most recent grave dated from 1429, and he seemed to remember that Vlad Tepes was born in 1428. It was hard to draw any conclusions from that.

He was about to open the door to the church, hoping to warm himself a little, when he heard a muffled sound, like a sob. He quickly ducked behind the nearest tombstone. An older man and a young woman came around the corner of the chapel in the other direction. They were wearing furs, and the damp marks on their coats suggested that they had been kneeling in front of one of the graves. The man's face was severe; the young woman's was buried in a handkerchief. When she put it away, Sam's heart stopped, for she was incredibly beautiful. Large dark blue eyes, very pale skin, a fine nose, a beautifully shaped mouth . . . He almost thought he saw something of Alicia Todds about her — his Alicia!

The man put his arm around her shoulders. "Don't cry, Yser. It was God's will."

Sam watched them walk toward the gate, wondering what he should do. Approach them? Ask them about the date and location? About Vlad Tepes's castle? The problem was, he wasn't exactly presentable in his white linen pajamas, especially at this temperature. Maybe it would be better to follow them at a distance and wait for an opportunity to talk to them.

At that moment shouts arose from the wood around the cemetery: "Get them! Yeah, get 'em!"

Three boys about Sam's age ran out of the trees. The girl cried out, and her father swore. "Blasted hooligans!"

Were they being robbed? Sam didn't hesitate. He stood up and grabbed a rock from the path. The boys had jumped the old man and were hitting him with sticks.

"Take this, you old goat! Here, take this!"

In two steps Sam came up behind the first boy and hit him hard on the back of his neck. The young man collapsed in a heap, dropping his club. The others turned to face him.

"Where did you come from, you little turd?" Though he barely reached Sam's shoulder, the taller of the two rushed forward, not anticipating a block from Sam. Clearly he'd never had the benefit of Master Yaku's lessons! Through judo, Sam had learned to turn the energy and power of an opponent's attack back against him. Thus, instead of falling back, he raised his arm and thrust out his hip to protect himself. The surprised thief slammed into his thigh and did a somersault into the snow, which Sam followed up with a good kick in the back. Without waiting for a reaction from the third robber, Sam seized the club from the ground and whirled it around his head as Master Yaku did in kendo training. The robber took a step backward, wide-eyed, then raced off toward the wood, soon joined by the taller of the boys. The third member of the trio lay facedown in the snow.

"Father!" the young woman exclaimed, rushing over to the man.

"My wrist," he said with a grimace. "They broke my wrist!"

She helped him to his feet while Sam checked the robber's breathing. He was only knocked out and would pull through with nothing worse than a good headache.

"Dirty little thieves," roared the old man. "Without you, my boy —" He examined Sam with a mixture of gratitude and astonishment. "It was God's grace that put you on our path! But, may one ask, what happened for you to be so ill clothed?"

"I . . . I was attacked too," Sam lied. "There were more of them, and they stole my clothes."

"In that case, help yourself to this fellow's clothing. That would only be fair!"

"It's cold," answered Sam, who could feel his toes becoming stiff. "If I take his clothes . . ."

"Forget your scruples, my boy! His accomplices are probably watching from somewhere behind these trees. As soon as we leave, they'll get him to shelter."

Sam hesitated, but yielded to the old man's arguments. He took the robber's boots and woolen jacket, but left him his heavy sweater and pants.

"Now, that's more reasonable," said the man in the fur coat. "And while I can't shake hands with you, let me at least introduce myself: Baltus, Hans Baltus of the image-makers' guild. I am forever obliged to you. And this is my daughter, Yser."

The girl nodded gently, without ceasing to support her father. Close up, she was even prettier. A few blond curls had escaped from her hat, and she had a mischievous glint in her eyes. But then she looked away, as was proper in the presence of a stranger.

Baltus seemed to notice Sam's turmoil, because he spoke up

more loudly: "Let's not stay here, my young friend. Those rascals may go get reinforcements. Are you heading into town?"

"Er, yes. Into town, yes."

"In that case, it would be our pleasure to invite you to supper! We owe you that at least, don't we?"

Leaving the robber behind, they followed the muddy path that wound through the forest. Hans Baltus put his wrist in a sling made from his daughter's scarf, while railing against bandits of all sorts.

"The moment you go beyond the city walls, you're no longer safe! This marriage is to blame too. I shouldn't complain about it, but there are so many men-at-arms in Bruges that all the rogues have fled. So now they're roaming the countryside, on the lookout for the first traveler they find!"

Bruges, thought Sam. The name didn't mean anything to him. Was Vlad Tepes's castle in Bruges? He took a deep breath. The air tasted almost salty.

"You may well ask," continued Baltus, "why I would risk going beyond the ramparts. This cemetery is quite far away, I know. But my poor wife was very attached to this place. She used to come often when she was a child; her grandmother is buried here. And it's been a year today since she was laid to rest here." He fell silent and heaved a sigh, and Yser again took refuge in her handkerchief.

"I'm very sorry," murmured Sam.

"But what about you?" Baltus asked. "Did you come to visit someone who passed away?"

"In a way, yes."

"In a way?"

By now, Sam was used to these kinds of questions, and

knew to make up a vague story that might earn him some sympathy without attracting suspicion.

"I can't say that I really knew her — she was a distant cousin of my father. Her name was Marga Waagen. I don't have any family anymore, so I came to Bruges to see her."

"Old Marga? She died several months ago! Didn't you know?"

"I just found out today." This at least was true: Sam had just read her name on a tombstone!

"As far as I know, she lived alone and she wasn't very rich," added Baltus. "You won't find any of her descendants here. She came from the east, I believe, from Malines, is that right?"

"From Malines, exactly. That's where I'm from too."

"You come from Malines, you learn of your aunt's death, and on top of that you get attacked! What a terrible series of events!"

"Yes, that's pretty much it."

They reached the edge of the wood, and the city suddenly materialized before Sam's dazzled eyes: a sweep of stone dotted with a thousand snow-covered roofs, surrounded by water and windmills on every side. Bruges seemed suspended between the darker sky and the far-off horizon of the sea. Two large buff-bowed boats with rectangular sails seemed to be gliding right up to the walls, escorted by wheeling seagulls. Colored fabric hung from the ramparts of the city, and blazing torches lit the intense activity on the outer harbor. Workmen unloaded barrels and baskets with contents destined to resupply the city. Curiously, this bustle was taking place almost without any sound, as if muffled by the heavy white mantle of snow. *A frozen mirage,* thought Sam. *A winter illusion.*

But as they approached the first bridge, the hubbub grew

and took on a life of its own. They passed under a fortified gate and blinked in the glare from the torches. Dozens of men were unloading the goods from a ship that was all timbers and lines onto smaller vessels, with an astonishing economy of words and gestures. Only a few foremen spoke:

"Faster, men! The count wants this game in his kitchens at eight o'clock! There's a wedding banquet tonight!"

"My herrings, you clumsy oafs! Carry my herrings properly!"

"Thirty bales of cloth to unload! I need ten porters!"

They made their way between the barrels and bales, and reached a longboat just as it was casting off. Baltus hailed the skipper. "Ahoy, master pilot! I am Hans Baltus of the image-makers' guild. I need to be dropped off with my family at the Saint Anne wharf. Is that on your way?"

"The image makers have my deepest respect," said the man with a bow. "Come aboard. I will take you to Saint Anne!"

They settled themselves as best they could amid the cargo while the sailor and his son put their poles in the water and pushed out into the canal. Sitting on one of the barrels, Baltus whispered to Sam, "I don't believe you told me your name."

"Er, Samuel . . . Samuel Waagen."

"And is this the first time you've come to Bruges, Samuel?"

"I hoped to get some help from my aunt."

"In other words, you don't know anybody here."

Sam jumped at the opening. "Before he died, my father mentioned a certain Vlad Tepes who lived around here. But I don't know where."

"Vlad Tepes? I've never heard speak of him. But it's not as if we lack strangers: The English bring us their wool, the Italians buy it, the Germans do business of all sorts, the French and the Spanish always come to our fairs, and then there are the Burgundians, of course, who are part of the count's retinue. But Vlad Tepes, that's a name I don't recognize."

Sam slumped on his barrel. He had suspected for some time now that he was at neither the right place nor the right period, and Baltus had just confirmed his fears. Bruges was clearly in Western Europe, whereas Wallachia was much farther to the east. And even if, by some miracle, he managed to get there, he was arriving twenty-five or thirty years too soon. Vlad Tepes would still be just a baby!

"My house is yours for as long as you need to decide what to do next," the old man offered. "There is work here for a diligent boy, especially with these festivities. You've heard that Count Philip is in Bruges and that he has gotten married, haven't you?"

"Well, that is . . . I haven't paid very much attention."

"To Isabel of Portugal. They held the ceremony last week. The entire city is celebrating, and if you stay, you can enjoy the tournaments and all the free food! But as for beds, I fear there aren't any to be had within five leagues. So you will do just as well staying with me."

As the boat went up the canal, it drifted by a square from which music and laughter could be heard.

"Everything happens there, on the great squares of the city center," said the old man, shaking his head. "Too many people, too much noise. Luckily my daughter and I live a little out of the way. Come, here we are."

"Saint Anne!" announced the sailor.

They stepped onto the wharf, which was slippery and poorly lit. Baltus complained of the pain in his wrist. "Those scoundrels have almost cost me an arm! And this is exactly the wrong time for it! Come on, let's hurry. We need a warm fire."

They walked along a cold alleyway to Baltus's house, where they were greeted by a servant woman as wide as the door. She didn't seem pleased to welcome Sam, and barely grumbled a good evening. For his part, he was surprised by the strong smell that filled the house. It was like camphor or eucalyptus, or the salve that Grandma rubbed on her chest when she had bronchitis.

"Bonne, prepare the bed near the studio for this young man."

"Is he a new apprentice?" the maid asked with a touch of annoyance.

"You can consider him as such. But first, serve us dinner in front of the fireplace; we're frozen through! And bring me a bandage; I have to wrap this arm before it swells too much."

Yser led the servant woman to the stairs, explaining the encounter at the cemetery and Sam's situation. Baltus asked Sam to follow him. "Come this way, my boy. I'll show you your nest. It isn't big, but it's better than sleeping out of doors."

Baltus led him down a hallway to a door topped with a coat of arms that showed three kneeling men bowing to a fourth, who stood with his hand outstretched.

"Those are the arms of the guild of image makers," Baltus explained. "The man on the right is Saint Luke, our patron. He is blessing the three representatives of the trade: the mirror maker, the illuminator, and the painter. You see the mirror, the book, and the brushes? Tools of our trades. For my part," he added with pride, "I belong to the third group, the most noble one, the painters."

Sam, who was chilled to the bone, felt a wave of warmth filling him. Image makers, as in people who created pictures! He had stumbled across a painter!

"That's extraordinary," he burst out.

"Isn't it?" said Baltus in agreement. "Do you like painting?"

"I . . . yes!"

"In that case, let's go in!"

He pushed the door open, and the medicinal smell became stronger still. There was a long table covered with pots, paintbrushes, mortars to grind the pigments, and various tools to prepare the panels. A high window was flanked by two easels, one of which carried an unfinished portrait of Yser. To the right, where the smells were the strongest, stood a kind of stove with pots of different sizes filled with thick black liquids.

"Those are my varnishes," explained Baltus. "My secret recipes! The painting I am working on, over there, is a portrait of my daughter. The count has organized a contest to choose which member of the guild will have the honor of painting his young bride. I dare to hope that this modest work will attract his attention."

"Beautiful," Sam breathed, thinking more of the model than her representation.

"I'm glad you think so. Particularly since there is a pretty sum involved that would greatly help my affairs, provided I can finish all this in time . . . Ah, here we are," he continued, as he walked toward the back of the studio.

He opened the door to a small room in the back. It was apparently used for storage, with stacked-up furniture and a bed under a round skylight.

"Don't worry, the maid will straighten this up for you.

This is where I lodged my apprentices when the studio was busier. Since my wife's death, I haven't had the heart to train young people as much. . . . Now I spend more time mixing pigments and oils than standing in front of my easel! That's why this contest is so important to me. I need to prove that Hans Baltus isn't finished — and prove it to myself as well! And I think I may be fairly close to succeeding," he whispered conspiratorially.

Just then, Yser entered the studio, carrying a stoneware pot and a linen bandage.

"For your arm, Papa. I also brought some liniment for your muscles."

Sam watched as Yser cared for her father, fascinated by her unnerving resemblance to Alicia Todds. She had taken off her hat, and her blond hair cascaded down to her shoulders. Her face wasn't quite the same; her eyes were less almond-shaped; but as for the rest — the color of the eyes, the delicate shape of her nose, the laughing mouth, and the very white teeth — it was enough to make Sam's head spin!

During the supper that followed — boiled mutton with carrots and peasant bread — Sam deliberately remained silent. This was mostly out of caution, because he didn't want to reveal or betray himself; but he also wanted to observe Yser at his leisure, without worrying about the ebb and flow of conversation. She didn't say much either, content to nod as her father told his stories, and seeming to avoid turning toward Sam.

At the end of the meal he decided to ask the question that had preoccupied him as soon as he realized he was in the wrong time. "You spoke of work earlier. Do you have any idea where I might get some?"

"At the wine harbor, for sure. They always have barrels to be loaded. I will show you the place tomorrow if you like."

"And they pay well? I mean in good coins?"

"Good, good — they pay you like a porter, in proportion to the task performed! But I warn you, they start at six o'clock there, and you'd best go to bed early if you don't want to miss the hiring. I'll wake you at dawn if that suits you. At my age one gets up early in any case."

Sam thanked Baltus and gave Yser a smile that he hoped was full of warmth. Once in his room, he undressed and put on the old nightclothes the servant had laid on the bed. As he slipped under the blanket, he considered the best way to find the coin that would allow him to return home. Bruges appeared to be a large city, nothing like the monastery at Iona or the village of Set Maat. So finding a coin shouldn't be too difficult, but the *right* coin . . .

As he thought about it, he realized that on his three previous trips, the coin had never been very far from the stone statue. On Iona it was hidden in a cave only a few hundred feet from Colm Cille's cove; Corporal Chartrel had been wounded a few houses away from the statue; and Setni's son, Ahmosis, had been touring the tomb, the scarab on his finger, when Sam appeared. Perhaps then it was necessary for the coin — or the medal or jewel — to be close to the stone statue in order to activate it? That if the two were not brought together within a given area, it wasn't possible to time-travel? That would suggest the coin he needed was hidden somewhere near the cemetery. Or with the robbers. Or with Baltus and his daughter . . . but that wasn't certain. Maybe all the coins in Bruges had holes in them. Or some of them, at least. He would know for sure tomorrow.

Sam was about to blow out his candle and go to sleep when he remembered Lily's phone. He pulled it from the pants pocket where he had carefully stowed it: THURSDAY, JUNE 10, 6:37 P.M. — barely an hour later. An hour of his own time had passed for the six or seven hours that he had actually spent in Bruges. The phone was still measuring the time he started from!

He went through the various menus to see if they held any other surprises. Internet, games, photographs, movies, ringtones, instant messaging, calculator, calendar, GPS. . . . Rudolf must have spent a small fortune on it. Sam tried the GPS — it might indicate his exact position — but the locator software didn't work; after all, this was six centuries before the invention of satellites! He accidentally set off the ringtone — *He makes my heart skip a beat / Oh yes* — and had to bury the phone under the covers. All he needed was for Baltus to walk in asking him for the name of the group and the title of the single! The song lyrics sounded odd to his ears, as if he'd almost become a stranger to his mother tongue; his brain had gotten remarkably used to the sounds of *kerk, brugge, zwyn,* etc., which he had been hearing all afternoon. One of the many mysteries of Egyptian magic, no doubt.

He then checked out the gallery of digital photos stored in the phone. This was nosy of him, but the circumstances required it. Most of the snapshots were of his cousin's favorite stuffed animal, a kind of floppy dog with clipped gray fur she called Zan. She had taken his picture in every possible position: Zan with his head down and his ears hanging; Zan wearing a plastic bag and a rain hat; Zan sitting on the toilet. Sam couldn't help but smile; at that moment he would have given a lot to hug Zan himself. There were also three self-portraits of Lily taken from too close and poorly framed, distorting her cheeks and nose. Sam could feel tears in his eyes. *Lily* . . .

He shut the phone; best not to let the blues get the better of him. Besides, he thought he heard a noise by the front door. He got up and tiptoed across the studio, candle in hand. It must be past midnight; everybody was supposed to be asleep. Holding his breath, he stepped into the hallway. Nothing suspicious. He went as far as the door: the bolt was pulled back. To let somebody in or to go out? At this time of night, and with all this snow . . . Sam gently turned the handle and glanced outside.

Footprints led away from the house and down the deserted street.

CHAPTER THIRTEEN

The Hamsters of Bruges

"Samuel . . . Samuel Waagen!"

Sam was very far away, deep in an abyss of fatigue and sleepiness. Opening his eyes required a superhuman effort.

"It's time, my boy!"

It took Sam a couple of seconds to recognize the face of the man leaning over him, holding a candle. Baltus . . . Yser . . . Bruges . . .

"Get up! You're going to miss the hiring!"

"The hiring," Sam repeated mechanically. In the end he got up, dressed, and joined the old man in the darkened dining room. A steaming pot sat on the table, along with slices of dried ham, cheese, and a loaf of white bread. A good fire blazed in the fireplace. Without asking, Baltus served him a black and aromatic liquid in a metal mug.

"Drink this. It will warm you up."

Sam swallowed a mouthful of what seemed to be burned coffee with a cinnamon aftertaste. It was strange, but not unpleasant. "How does your wrist feel?" he asked.

Baltus waved his bandaged hand. "It's causing me pain and

I hope it isn't broken. I'm going to take advantage of the trip to town to see my doctor."

"Are you going to be able to continue painting?" Sam slipped some ham and cheese between two pieces of bread.

"I'll have to! The contest is in two days, so I must finish my daughter's portrait. You have a curious way of eating, Samuel Waagen," he added, seeing Sam tearing into his improvised sandwich.

"It's" — *chomp* — "a habit" — *chomp* — "I picked up in Malines," said Sam. He then remarked, "There's something strange in this business" — *chomp* — "I mean, about the robbers yesterday" — *chomp*. "What were they after, exactly?"

"Well, to rob me, I suppose! What do robbers want, except to steal things?"

"The people who stole my clothes were after something specific, from what they were saying. A coin with a hole in the middle, something like that."

He carefully observed Baltus's reaction, but the painter showed more amusement than interest.

"A hole in the middle? How much worth would that have, if the artisan who made it wouldn't even finish it? Be glad they were content to take your clothes. Thieves sometimes kill their victims, you know — so we really don't have much reason to complain, you and I."

Sam nodded. Baltus either didn't know anything about a coin with a hole in it, or he was a very good actor. Sam finished his sandwich and quickly slipped into the fur-collared coat that the painter saved for his apprentices, then followed him down the snowy street. The sun was gradually making its first appearance between the gray clouds. Everything was cold and still, like a fantastic movie set or a meticulous reconstruction of a medieval village, with high narrow houses, steep roofs, gothic decorations, and wooden beams projecting through the walls. They crossed a double-arched bridge under which swans were sleeping, beaks buried in their plumage, then passed through Bruges's inner walls to the heart of the city.

It was more densely built up than the Saint Anne neighborhood. The houses squeezed and pushed against one another, or seemed to tilt forward, the better to admire their reflections in the canal. The massive church bell tower, the pride of the city's inhabitants, rose above the faded roof tiles like a watchful sentinel. Baltus launched into the history of the tower's construction, but Sam, who was fascinated by everything he saw, hardly paid him any attention. They followed a series of deserted alleys, skirted a square covered with tents — home to the servants of the count's retinue, Baltus said — and finally reached the wine harbor.

The rest of Bruges might be resting after the festivities of the night, but the merchants and porters here were already busy preparing for the day's feasts. A dozen boats nosed gently at the dock, and men traded lively talk among the barrels.

Baltus approached a man with a red cap who was waving his staff in the air in great circles. "Hail there, harbormaster! One of my apprentices seeks something to do. Do you have any work to give him, in these days of the royal wedding?"

The harbormaster considered Sam with an expert eye. "He isn't built for loading, your apprentice. He's so skinny, he looks as if he hasn't eaten for a week! Here, try to lift this barrel."

He pointed to a barrel that a stocky fellow had just rolled onto the pavement. Sam bent down, wrapped his arms around it, and, trying to look casual, strained to lift it. He quickly gave up: It weighed as much as a dead donkey and wouldn't budge an inch. The porters nearby laughed uproariously.

"Looks as if your apprentice can barely lift his head!" joked the man in the red bonnet. "But if he doesn't have any arms, maybe he has legs. I am short one boy for the crane. The pay isn't as much, but he'll be better suited to the work."

Sam examined the strange wooden construction that stood over the left part of the wharf. It looked like a headless chicken, with a fat body and a neck that tapered as it rose higher. Though he had assumed it was scaffolding, it was in fact a wooden crane, whose great ropes lifted heavy cargo from the boats. As he watched, a boat pulled up alongside the crane, and the substantial tackle descended toward the deck.

"How much are you offering?" Baltus asked.

"Five deniers for the half day if he isn't too lazy," answered the harbormaster.

Baltus shot Sam a questioning look. Sam had no idea what five deniers represented, but rather than back out, he nodded yes.

"So it's agreed for a half day," concluded Baltus. "If the work suits him, he'll come back again this afternoon. You'll be able to find your way home, won't you, Waagen?"

Sam nodded again, said good-bye to Baltus, and listened carefully to the harbormaster's instructions as they walked around to the crane — or rather, to a huge drum mounted horizontally beneath it. Two boys stood inside the drum, walking in step, powering the crane by the simple friction of their feet. The harbormaster explained that the boys had to walk at the same pace, being careful not to get carried away by speed or to lose their balance when the drum slowed. Sam would join them, and if he proved worthy, he would be hired for the week.

Sam waited for the crane to stop and stepped into the cylinder. His two new companions greeted him with grunts, and he saw they were sweating in spite of the chill. At the boss's signal, all three started to trot in step.

"That's good, boys! All together!" cried the man in the red cap.

In the beginning it seemed almost easy: All Sam had to do was to match his pace to those of the two other *kranekinders,* or crane children. But after a quarter of an hour, he was distracted by the sound of the crane's mechanism, a complex interplay of ropes and pulleys that made a hellish noise above them. His shoe caught between two boards, and he felt the ground falling away from him before tumbling around like laundry in a washing machine. Luckily, the harbormaster called for a break right then. Sam's two companions caught their breath while he painfully got to his feet.

"This is the first time you turn, huh?" said one of the boys, whose eye was half closed, either by a wound or a deformity.

"That's right," said Sam, rubbing his back.

"You better be a little sharper if you don't want us to pocket your pay," he said with a nasty laugh.

"Yeah," the other one chimed in. "Things were different with Melchior. At least he could stay on his feet!"

The first boy shrugged. " 'Cept he's not coming back any time soon. He's got a hole in his head as big as a fist, and you can see his brains!"

Sam's ears immediately pricked up. "A hole in his head? What happened to him?"

"They say he got into a fight, or really that someone jumped him from behind. With a rock!"

"A rock," repeated Sam, thinking of the graveyard.

"Believe me, the pig who did that, if we get our mitts on him . . . See, he's got friends, Melchior!"

"I bet!" Sam said approvingly in the most detached tone he could achieve. "And he's at the hospital now?"

"At the hospital? Melchior? Why not with the sergeants of the watch while you're at it? No, like we told you, he has lots of pals."

The half-blind boy shot Sam a hostile glance — a hostile half-glance, actually.

"So you'd like to look at his brains too?"

"Oh no, not me," Sam said hastily. "I was just making conversation."

"Then you'd better save your breath. There's another barge to unload."

The harbormaster snapped his fingers, and the three *krane-kinders* resumed their endless, absurd walk inside the drum. Sam felt as if he were in a giant hamster wheel. The hamsters of Bruges!

After three or four hours of this regime, he was finally able to escape the stupid wheel. The morning's work was ending, there were no more boats to unload, all the barrels had been picked up, and last but not least, his legs and toes had turned to mush. He let his two companions collect their pay first, then dragged himself over to the man in the red cap. The man frowned.

"You're lucky those two know what they're doing, otherwise I wouldn't have kept you. You're too slow and clumsy! I gave each of them an extra denier for their trouble. One of your deniers, of course!"

He stuck his hand in his pocket and pulled out three pathetic metal disks. Sam accepted the coins, but he was less disappointed by the man's obvious ill will than by the absence of a hole in the coins' centers.

"Wait! If I come back this afternoon, can I have another coin? A coin with a hole in it, say? Even if I have to work for several days?"

The harbormaster seemed baffled.

"A coin with a hole? Why would you want a coin with a hole? You must not be from around here. Neither the Bruges sol nor the denier has ever had a hole! Much less the livre! If you're looking for counterfeits, you should go see the money changers. Those people handle every coin imaginable!"

"The money changers?"

"Yes, the money changers on the Place de la Bourse! Don't tell me you don't know the money changers either?" His tone was getting suspicious.

"The money changers," exclaimed Sam. "Of course! Place de la Bourse! How stupid of me!"

The harbormaster sighed and turned to answer one of his porters' questions. For a moment Sam was tempted to catch up with the two *kranekinders* and ask them again about this Melchior — probably the very boy he had knocked out at the cemetery; but they could easily suspect something and wind up turning against him.

Instead Sam headed in the direction of the bell tower, which rang every quarter hour, and asked an old lady wrapped in a shawl for the way to the Place de la Bourse. As he walked along, he saw that the city was now fully awake. The streets were jammed with a dense crowd of men, dogs, and horses making their way by fits and starts around carts and gossiping porters. Good humor reigned in spite of the snow, and passersby talked enthusiastically about the banquets and the jousts they had seen the day before, and the free bread and meat they hoped for today. From a distance, Sam glimpsed the fenced-in arena with its pennants, where the tournaments were being held, but he didn't see any knights in armor waiting to take their turns. . . . Too bad.

The money-changers' district was just as crowded. The rectangular Place de la Bourse was lined with imposing houses with grilled windows and crenellated roofs. Trestle tables stood in front of each façade, with little awnings to protect them from the rain. Vigorous arguments raged on both sides of the tables, and it took Sam a while to understand what was going on.

Bruges attracted merchants from the four corners of Europe, each using a different currency. The money changers converted these currencies into Bruges livres, sols, and deniers, so merchants from different countries could buy one another's goods. The problem was reaching an agreement on the exact value of the currencies. The merchants always demanded more and the changers always offered less, which explained the outbursts of voices all around. One of the money changers, who spoke with a pronounced Italian accent, was a particularly gifted performer.

"At that price, Cortés, I'll wind up sleeping in a barn! Have you thought of my children?"

"Pull the other one, Bartolomeo," answered the man called

Cortés. "You're the fattest banker on the Bruges square. Give me what I'm asking or I'll take my business elsewhere!"

"Ah, Cortés, *Madonna!* You're tearing my heart out. You're my friend and I want to satisfy you, but I'm nearly dead! See how my blood is bleeding? My tears are flowing?"

He turned to the young man seated behind him, who had a marked board and tokens resting on his knees.

"Enzo, *presto!* Please calculate 15,625 divided by 125, less five livres for a commission, plus three as a rebate for Cortés."

Enzo apparently wasn't very fast. It took him a long time to get the answer, and Bartolomeo upbraided him: *"Ma Enzo!* Truly you are the stupidest idiot in the entire city! You aren't my nephew anymore, you're a calamity!"

When Enzo finally came up with a number, the money changer opened a box he kept at his feet and counted out the sum he named. Sam didn't have time to get a good look, but the cash box seemed to contain compartments and coins of all sizes. If only he could investigate it! But it was too late: Bartolomeo had already put his precious box under his bench. Sam strolled on by, looking casual, and took up a position behind a column farther on. For a long time he watched the banker carefully. There had to be some way for him to search that box!

CHAPTER FOURTEEN

Van Eyck's Secret

The Bruges bell tower had just rung three in the afternoon when Sam finally decided to go back to Saint Anne. In the meantime, he'd received two free apples and a loaf of bread in honor of the count's wedding, and bought a bag of smoked herring from a sidewalk vendor to go along with it. But the fish turned out to be incredibly salty, and he now felt so thirsty he could drink the canal dry.

The maid opened the door, scowling. "Don't make any noise. The master is receiving the constable."

"The constable?"

"Yes — the chief of police, if you prefer. He's here to see how the master is doing after yesterday's attack. Run along to your room so he doesn't see you!"

But Baltus must have heard, because he called to them from the living room. "Bonne? Is that our young man coming home?"

"At this very instant, sir," she said.

"Perfect! Bring him in. I want to introduce him to the constable."

The maid rolled her eyes but did so, and Sam was soon introduced to an imposing man wearing a carefully trimmed beard and a vest shot through with gold thread. He gave Sam a sharp look.

"So this is the boy who saved you, Master Baltus?" he asked in a deep, rumbling voice.

"I wouldn't be here if he hadn't miraculously appeared, messire."

"Miraculously, eh?" repeated the constable with an odd smile. "And what were you doing at the Vieux-Bois cemetery, young man?"

"I was praying at the grave of my aunt, Marga Waagen."

"Old Marga! I had a conversation with her at the fish market shortly before her death. She was deaf in one ear and had lost half her teeth. Did you know that?"

Sam sensed a trap. "I only knew her by name. She was a relative of my father's and I never met her. But I'm an orphan now, and I wanted to try my luck in Bruges."

"An orphan, eh? That's convenient," commented the constable. "Still, it seems you showed up at just the right time! Those robbers — what boldness! Do you know the story of Mertens the miller, Hans?" Baltus shook his head. "It happened eight or nine months ago, if I'm not mistaken," the constable continued. "Mertens had a misadventure much like yours — attacked by ruffians as he was leaving his mill. A passing traveler managed to drive them off. Naturally our Mertens thanks him, is enormously grateful, gives him room and board. One thing leads to another, and the man becomes his dearest friend. But three days later, our miller barely has his back turned when his 'savior' lets the thieves into the mill, where they steal every-thing!" He gave Sam a meaningful look. "You can't trust anyone, unfortunately!"

Baltus didn't appear to pick up the implication and merely offered a glass of German wine to his guest, who refused.

"Thank you very much, Hans. I only wanted to find out how you were doing and give your daughter this modest gift. I would have liked to have given it to her myself, but . . ."

"As I said, she went to visit her cousin. But she should be back soon."

"Unfortunately, my dear friend, the count is expecting me; I must oversee this evening's feast. So please give my respects to Miss Yser and have her let me know what she thinks of my present."

He stood up, clicked his heels, and bid farewell to the old man, while quite deliberately ignoring Sam.

"He's a good man, that constable," Baltus said after his departure. "He will be an excellent husband for Yser."

"A husband?" said Sam in a strangled voice. "But he's at least twice as old as she is!"

"Of course, but so what? He's been a widower for three years, and he's rich. He has a beautiful apartment in the Prinsenhof, the new palace that Count Philip is building in town. Who could ask for more? Yser is seventeen years old, an age where she should be settling down. As I told you, my affairs are not at their best, and there's no longer any chance of winning the prize money: My wrist is cracked and I can no longer hold my brushes. This marriage will assure Yser's security and her com-fort. She won't have to worry about anything anymore."

"But what about her? Does she agree?"

"Well, the constable is still a handsome man, isn't he? And attentive too. Look at what he made for her, with his own hands!"

He pointed to a wrought-iron candelabra on the table. It was shaped more or less like a tree, its branches twisting into holders for three candles. Sam was not impressed.

"In addition to being an artist of sorts," continued Baltus, "he's also a scientist. When police business leaves him a little respite, he works ardently at alchemy in the hope of making gold! Alchemists are cultivated people, you know, and deeply interested in sciences and the world. And he has not hidden the fact that if Yser becomes his wife, he will bring her in to share his efforts. Isn't it better to have a husband who opens the horizons of wisdom to his wife than some young idiot concerned only with giving her children? No, the constable is an excellent match and —"

At that moment, a burning smell wafted in from the hallway, and Baltus slapped his cheek. "Good God almighty! My oil preparation!"

He rushed to the studio and flung its door open. Black smoke rising from the stove had filled the room.

"The window! Let in some fresh air!"

Sam ran to the window, and after wrestling with the latch, managed to open it enough to create a draft. Baltus's brew smelled like old burnt socks and sore-throat salve.

"What was I thinking?" cried Baltus. "I completely forgot my experiment! I'm no longer good for anything, neither painting nor experimenting!"

He picked up the cauldron with a cloth and, holding it at arm's length, threw the mix out into the gravel of the courtyard. "I almost had it! I'm sure I almost had it!"

"Was it . . . was it so important?" hazarded Sam.

"Two years, my boy! For two years now, I've been trying to pierce Van Eyck's secret! If I could only get his mastery of oils, my paintings would sell so much better!"

Sam was unable to hide his surprise. "Van Eyck? You mean the painter?" Miss Delaunay had once told them about Van Eyck, but Sam hadn't realized he was connected with Bruges.

"Of course the painter, who else? He is Count Philip's favorite, and the count takes him everywhere. Some time ago he perfected a new technique to make his colors more lively and luminous, as if the light were literally coming out of the painting. The effect is striking, and his portraits are admired by everyone. Each of his works sells for twenty times the price of mine!"

Sam was careful not to point out that Van Eyck might also have twenty times more talent. According to his teacher, he was one of the greatest artists of the Middle Ages.

"Last year," the old man continued, "one of his helpers let slip that Van Eyck obtains such perfect colors by adding a secret ingredient to his pigments and his oil. I have been trying to discover that substance ever since. I've spent whole nights at my stove, with all sorts of recipes! And I hadn't given up hope of succeeding. Unfortunately it's all ruined! But this is Van Eyck's fault as well! Instead of making such a mystery of it, why doesn't he share his discoveries with the guild?"

Baltus was so excited that he didn't notice Sam had turned pale. Van Eyck's secret . . . he knew Van Eyck's secret! Miss Delaunay had explained to them that although Van Eyck hadn't invented oil painting, he had revolutionized its use. To the ground-up pigments that provided the hues, and the oils that served to mix them, he added a substance that brought out the colors and made them easier to work with. And this mysterious substance was . . .

For the first time since the start of his "travels," Sam found himself facing a matter of conscience. Should he tell Baltus the secret that made Van Eyck so successful? Wouldn't that risk changing the course of history? There were lots of movies where changing a detail in the past had unforeseen repercussions on the future. What if that happened here? Sam hesitated. Of course everything would be very different if Baltus had lived *before* Van Eyck; revealing the great painter's techniques before he invented them might have been a disaster. But Baltus and Van Eyck were living at the same time; they even lived in the same city. Moreover, Baltus had been very generous to Sam; helping him in his research would be a way of thanking him. But he had to do it skillfully.

"Have you tried turpentine?"

"Ter . . . what?"

"Turpentine."

"You mean to say Venice turpentine."

"Er, yes. My grandfather said just turpentine."

"What does your grandfather have to do with it?"

Exactly what Sam was wondering too.

"Well, as it happens my grandfather did a bit of painting too."

"Your grandfather was a painter?"

"No, not really. He . . ." Sam noticed a clay pot sitting on the workbench where the brushes were stored. "He painted pots."

"Pots?"

"Well, vases. Yes, that's it, vases. He painted and decorated vases."

"By my faith, it's a curious idea, but not a bad one. And what's the connection with Venice turpentine?"

"My grandfather always told me: 'You see, Samuel, to make the colors luminous, you have to add a little turpentine.'"

"Venice turpentine," said Baltus thoughtfully. "After all, why not? It's a noble resin that could combine well with the colors. Of course we would have to determine its cooking temperature, but added to oil and the pigments it might help to bind them and give them a certain gloss . . . Venice turpentine! I hadn't thought of it, I must admit!"

The door to the street slammed and Yser shouted: "Papa? Papa? Is everything all right?"

"I'm in the studio, darling!"

The girl ran in, her cheeks reddened by the cold, apparently alarmed by the smell and the smoke. "Papa, what . . ."

"It's nothing," said Baltus reassuringly. "One of my preparations burned. But our friend here has made a suggestion of the very first importance. I'm going to the shop on the Grand-Place to buy some materials. In the meantime . . ." He looked at Sam, then at his daughter. "You told me you liked painting, didn't you, Mr. Waagen? You aren't clumsy, are you? Do you think you could finish this?" He pointed to the portrait of Yser on the easel.

"Me?"

"Yes, you! What have we got to lose? I won't be able to finish it myself for several days, and at that point it will be too late! The face, the hat, and the neck are complete; the hands and the folds of the dress are all that remain to be done. At worst, we'll keep it for ourselves, and if it's acceptable, we'll

try our luck. Who knows? You may have inherited your grandfather's talent."

Sam could hardly believe his ears. Baltus was suggesting
that he paint for real! And paint Yser to boot!

"I'm not sure I know how . . ."

"Come, come, we don't need that between us! I'm asking
you this as a favor. Yser, my beauty, don't make this young man
wait. Go put on your dress." The girl left the room. "See, my
colors are already on the palette; I prepared them earlier. You'll
just need to freshen them with some of this oil here. Use delicate strokes, especially for the hands. As for the dress itself,
that's the darkest part and you'll have no trouble. Just work
with caution and be sure not to go over what I've already done.
Remember, whatever happens, we have nothing to lose!"

Baltus snatched up his coat and ran from the room as if the
house were about to catch fire. Sam found himself alone in
the studio, uncertain as to what he should do. Examining the
portrait, he found it generally successful but not a work of real
genius. It had blank areas where the shapes were only sketched
in; he thought he could handle those. Sam had never worked
on a real canvas before, but since Baltus had urged him on . . .

Yser came downstairs after a few minutes, wearing a splendid black velvet dress. She sat down in a chair with golden arm-
rests, right in front of the easel, and assumed the pose without
a word or a smile. Sam carefully mixed his colors. He chose a
paintbrush, and when the orangish-pink paint was as pale as
he liked, he began to paint the girl's hands. His own hands
were trembling as he applied the first strokes, but he grew more
confident as the slim, delicate fingers gradually came to life on

the canvas. He even dared to look at Yser's face a few times, like a real painter trying to capture his model's expression. Her resemblance to Alicia Todds was still astonishing: a seventeen-year-old Alicia Todds, more mature and still more beautiful, with slightly rounder eyes and a more serious face. After a half hour of tense silence, she finally spoke.

"You really are a strange boy, Mr. Waagen. You burst out of the cemetery to save us, you put my father in a dither by giving him some recipe, and now you also know how to paint!"

Sam wasn't sure this was a compliment. "You seem as suspicious as the constable!" he said, trying to laugh it off.

"The constable? Did he come?"

"Yes, a while ago. I think he was looking for you. He even brought you a present."

Sam saw the girl's hands tense slightly.

"Your father told me you're going to marry him."

"That is his will," answered Yser more quietly.

"Is it not yours?"

"A girl must obey her father, mustn't she?"

There was as much warmth in her voice as in the canal's frozen waters. Sam didn't press the point. He rinsed his brush and added a drop of oil to the dark colors on the palette. He needed a deep black that would still suggest the velvet of the dress — a somewhat thick black, verging on plum.

"Are you going to stay with us for a long time?" Yser asked after a pause.

Occupied with his colors, Sam took a moment to answer. "Don't worry, I'll leave as quickly as I can. Just as soon as I earn a little money."

"By turning the crane?"

"If I don't find any other way."

"The *kranekinder* have a terrible reputation. Some of them are no better than thieves."

So she too thought him in league with the cemetery robbers! He looked her directly in the face. "I'd like to point out that it was *your father* who suggested I join the *kranekinder*. I've just come to Bruges and I don't know anybody. And especially not the people who attacked your father yesterday, if that's what you want to know."

Yser hesitated before answering.

"I'm willing to believe you, Sam," she said.

Baltus was in a state of high excitement. He had spent the three hours since dinner pacing around his studio, feeding wood to the fire, adding a little oil and then a little turpentine to the pot on the stove, and mixing the whole with the delicate touch of a master chef. The smell was so revolting that he'd had to leave the windows open despite the Arctic chill. Sam, his fingers stiff with cold and his collar turned up to his nose, was doing his best to appear attentive, though his sole desire was to go to sleep. But he had one more task to accomplish that night, and it would have been impolite to show his impatience.

"There we are!" said Baltus enthusiastically. "Look at the color of this paste! And the smoothness! I think I've got it! Bring me the glass bottle, please."

Sam did so, moving like a zombie. The old man set the bottle on a corner of the stove and put a funnel in its neck. Then he carefully poured in the contents of the pot, an amber-colored liquid whose vapors stung the eyes.

"There! We're going to let the preparation cool until

tomorrow. I'll filter it once and cook it a second time, and then I'll make a first attempt with paint. And if it's God's wish . . . but I have bored you enough for one evening, my boy! It's time for us to go to bed."

He covered the bottle with a damp cloth and began to blow out the candles as Sam closed the window.

"Good night, Samuel Waagen," he said. "And thank you for the Venice turpentine!"

Sam pretended to head for his room, but as soon as the old painter's light had disappeared up the stairs, he turned back into the studio. He needed a tool that could cut cloth or leather. Not finding any scissors, he took two pointed knives from the workbench. The portrait of Yser looked a bit lugubrious in the gloom, but Sam felt proud of the hands nonetheless. You might almost have thought that Baltus himself had done them. Almost . . .

Once on his bed, he took Lily's cell phone from its hiding place above a beam and looked at the date: THURSDAY, JUNE 10, 11:11 P.M. Only six hours had passed in his own time. That was still reasonable, though Grandma would be worried, and Lily would certainly have to act concerned. Above all, he hoped that she hadn't stopped thinking about him!

Sam then concentrated on the cell phone's functions. He had several projects for the next day. First, he wanted to take some photographs of the city. Bruges in the snow in 1430 — a worldwide scoop, guaranteed! He would have to work discreetly, of course; if he were caught with modern electronics, he was sure to be thrown into prison or burned at the stake.

He undressed and examined the jacket he had "borrowed" the day before from one of the robbers — Melchior, according to the conversation of the two *kranekinders*. The coat was leather with a wool lining. He wanted to cut a kind of pocket for the mobile phone, with a small opening so Sam could use it without being seen. If need be, he could ask the maid for a needle and thread in the morning.

As Sam examined the inside of the garment, looking for the best place to cut, he came across a nearly invisible slit under the left sleeve. The coat already had its own pocket! He slipped two fingers inside the lining. The space was big enough to store the phone, as long as he enlarged the upper part and . . .

Suddenly he felt paper under his fingers — a tiny paper cylinder. He took it out into the light and unrolled it. It was very badly written, almost illegible, and Sam had to read it several times before he could understand it:

> *In God's name, amen. January 7, at Bruges. The bearer to receive from my account with the banker Grimaldi 3 livres and 12 sols, payable from the 11th, without action on my part and against good performance. May God keep you always.*

There was also a signature, but it was even less legible than the rest. What could the message mean? It involved money, a banker Grimaldi, a bearer — was that like a porter at the wine harbor? — action, performance . . . and it was all going on right now. Had Melchior stolen this paper in hopes of earning a few coins with it? In any case, Sam intended to return to the Place de la Bourse the next day. If the situation involved a banker, he could learn more about it there. And he had another idea as well. . . .

Sam yawned so wide he almost popped his jaw out of joint. He had found the pocket at just the right time; it would save him a few precious minutes. Using the sharper of the two knives, he cut a window into the leather, about an inch and a half square. This would allow him to take some candid photographs of the city without fear of being spotted. If the shots weren't good, he could just take them over again — the magic of the twenty-first century! He put the knife and phone aside and huddled under the blankets to sleep.

CHAPTER FIFTEEN

Three Livres and Twelve Sols

The next morning, Sam took a deep breath. *Nothing ventured, nothing gained*, he told himself firmly.

He strode across the Place de la Bourse and made his way through the crowd of merchants and shoppers. The weather had warmed a little, and the snow was beginning to melt in the street, brewing a muddy soup stirred by people's boots and clogs. As many people crowded the town as ever, and Sam had finally seen knights in armor on the tournament grounds, surrounded by squires and heralds blowing trumpets and praising their great deeds. The colorful helmets and shields gleamed in the noonday sun, and Sam was impressed by the horses' size and metal armor. When the riders collided in jousts, their lances sometimes shattered with ominous cracks, and the fighters tumbled to the ground, raising clouds of dust and mud before hacking away at each other with swords. Despite the shoving, Sam managed to take three or four photos of the mêlée from the inside of his coat. But he hadn't lingered, because he had better things to do.

Once under the awnings of the Place de la Bourse, he had

no trouble spotting Bartolomeo the money changer: He was the one who talked the loudest. His nephew was still at his left, head bowed over the counting board. Sam waited until a new customer showed up, then slipped his hand in his coat and switched the phone to calculator mode. He was about to gamble part of his future.

After the usual politenesses, the two men began to bargain. The merchant was a short, bald man who had come to Bruges to buy cloth and wanted to change 642 Venetian ducats into Bruges livres and sols. From what Sam had seen the day before, and a little he'd learned from Baltus, he knew that the livre was worth twenty sols and the sol was worth twelve deniers, which meant the livre was worth 240 deniers. That complicated things a little for Sam, who was used to counting in tens rather than twelves, but he had been practicing.

"One sol and five deniers to the ducat," offered Bartolomeo.

"One sol and seven deniers," the other demanded.

"Do you want me to have to close up shop? Go bankrupt between now and the next fair? *Madonna!* One sol and six deniers to the ducat, Gabriel. I can't do better than that."

"Agreed," grumbled the other man.

"Enzo, *per piacere!* Do 642 ducats at one sol and six deniers to the ducat."

The nephew began manipulating his tokens, while Sam, his head half hidden by his coat — thank goodness for the lighted screen — pushed buttons frantically. *One sol is worth 12 deniers*, he thought, *so 1 sol and 6 deniers equals 1.5 sols. 642 ducats times 1.5 sols equals 963 sols. One livre is worth 20 sols, so if I divide 963 by 20, I get 48.15 livres in 642 ducats. I store the 48 in memory, leaving 0.15 livres to be converted to sols. One livre equals 20 sols, so 0.15 livres equals 0.15 times 20 sols, equals 3 sols.* This was the sort of mental gymnastics he had been practicing all morning. *How many livres was that again? Press* MEMORY: 48.

"It's forty-eight livres and three sols," he announced loudly.

The calculation had taken him about forty seconds all told. Intrigued, Bartolomeo and his customer turned to look at him.

"That's forty-eight livres and three sols," Sam repeated. "I assure you."

Unnerved by this unexpected competition, Enzo had to redo the calculation twice before being able to confirm the result, at least two minutes later.

"Er, yes, Uncle. It's forty-eight livres and three sols. That's right."

Bartolomeo stared at Sam without saying anything, then briskly took his cash box from under the bench and paid the cloth buyer. No sooner he had done so than a second merchant appeared, wanting to convert 300 Portuguese reals into Bruges currency. This time the discussion was even livelier — Bartolomeo threatened to slit his wrists — before the two men could agree on the exchange rate: one real for thirty-five deniers.

"Enzo," said Bartolomeo, watching Sam out of the corner of his eye. "Do three hundred reals at thirty-five deniers to the real."

Sam didn't waste a second: 300 reals times 35 deniers was 10,500 deniers. Since one livre was worth 240 deniers, 10,500 deniers were the equivalent of 10,500 divided by 240, or 43.75 livres. For the decimal fractions, repeat the same calculation as before: one livre equals 20 sols, so 0.75 livre equals 0.75 times 20 . . . 15 sols.

"It's forty-three livres and fifteen sols," Sam declared proudly.

Poor Enzo, who was clearly rattled, took an interminable length of time to reach the same result. Once the customer had left, Bartolomeo spoke directly to Sam. "What exactly are you after, boy?"

"Work," Sam answered immediately.

"You mean doing calculations?"

"Exactly."

"But you have a secret, right?"

Sam had anticipated the question. He displayed the inside of his woolen coat, on which he had drawn a charcoal grid with an impressive series of random numbers.

"I have my own system. I count on my fingers and I use this."

"Suppose I asked you 543 times 956?"

Sam repeated his business, hidden under his coat: "That's 519,108," he said almost instantly.

Bartolomeo examined him thoughtfully, then suddenly seemed to make up his mind. "Enzo, why don't you go look at the tournaments a little, no? There are knights from Italy today. You can return when the belfry rings the fifth hour, *capito?*"

His nephew didn't need to be asked twice. Passing behind Sam to yield him his place on the bench, he whispered: "Thank you! Come back every afternoon if you feel like it!"

Sam sat down in front of the board with the tokens, leaning sideways against the wall so he'd be able to manipulate the phone without being seen. Step one was a success.

"Enzo is my nephew. He's a good calculator, but he's as slow as a slug! I no longer have the eyes of twenty years ago, and I need a helper. If I had somebody like you every day . . ." He began to speak more softly, so the other money changers wouldn't hear him. "How much are you asking for, boy?"

"My rate . . ." Sam began. "I'm looking for a particular coin. A coin with a hole in the middle. Would you have that?"

Bartolomeo scratched his head. He bent to pick up his cash box and rummaged in it for a moment.

"I think I got a couple from a seller of furs. I was being kind that day, but I bit my fingers over it afterward. Nobody wants coins from Hungary or any of those places." He showed the coins to Sam: two metal disks of a dull, sad orange — perhaps some kind of copper. They seemed to be the right size, and above all, they had holes in their centers. Bingo!

"If you do a good job, you can have both of them, boy."

Sam shivered: All his guesses thus far had been right! The coins were indeed with the money changer! A few more calculations and . . .

Just then a new client approached, holding a leather purse in his hand. He emptied it onto the counter. "I have a thousand florins for you, Bartolomeo," he said. "I want a good price for them, and fast — before the weavers' hall closes!"

The day was spent in a hundred multiplications, another hundred divisions, dozens of additions and subtractions, and a few percentages. Sam had never put so much energy into math! Mrs. Cubert would have been proud. He had problems on one or two occasions — with the Strasbourg gros in particular — but Bartolomeo had proved patient, explaining to him that Rome wasn't built in a day — *in un giorno*, to be exact. Sam's prowess had even wound up attracting a few curious spectators who applauded the speed of his answers. No doubt about it, he had a brilliant career as a "calculator" ahead of him . . . at least as long as the phone's battery lasted.

But after a while, there were fewer and fewer merchants,

and Bartolomeo decided they were finished for the day. He asked Sam to come back the next day, holding out the glitter of more extraordinary coins (probably ones he was trying to get rid of), but Sam was evasive. When he had the two metal disks in his hands and felt confident that they would fit the stone statue, he asked the money changer for one last favor.

"I have a piece of paper that I wanted to show you, Messire Bartolomeo. It was given to me, but I don't understand it all." He held out the message he found in Melchior's secret pocket. Bartolomeo adjusted his spectacles on his nose and read:

"'In God's name . . . January 7 . . . The bearer to receive from my account with the banker Grimaldi 3 livres and 12 sols . . . May God keep you always.' This is a bearer note."

"A bearer note?"

"*Si.* The one who wrote the note has an account with the banker Grimaldi, and the other one, the person he gave the note to, can get three livres and twelve sols from him after the 11th."

"And the bearer?"

"The bearer? *But*, it's you! You're the one who's bearing the note, no?"

"You mean to say that if I go to the banker Grimaldi, I will get the money?"

"*Si*, but there are two conditions: that the person signing the note has not taken action to revoke the order, and that you have executed the mission that was asked of you."

"The mission?"

"The mission, *certo!* It's written in the note: 'against good performance.' The banker will pay as soon as the mission is executed and the one giving the order has not changed his mind. If you did not do a good job, the person writing the order will tell Grimaldi not to pay. Isn't that what you expected?"

"Er, yes, of course. But it's a little complicated for me."

"And the work, what did it consist of?"

"Calculations. Lots of calculations. But why pay me with this kind of letter instead of real coins?"

"Bearer notes allow merchants to pay people who are far away. I write notes to Rome, I send them to you, and you have someone give you the money at Bruges. That way, the money doesn't travel, only the paper. It's less dangerous."

"And this banker Grimaldi. Where would one meet him?"

Bartolomeo pointed. "Right across the way!"

Sam thanked him and walked across the square, clutching his coins. Perhaps he could claim the money and buy a gift for Baltus and Yser, to thank them for all their help. Soon he stood before a table piled with thick books. A lean old man sat hidden behind them.

"The young gentleman desires?" asked Grimaldi with a pinched smile. Sam put the bearer note on the table. The less he said, the fewer problems he would attract. Long fingers, stained and wrinkled as old parchment, seized the paper, and two suspicious eyes looked it over, gleaming with interest at the signature.

"Ah, you come on behalf of Mr. Klugg. Very good!"

Sam didn't know Mr. Klugg from Adam, but he nodded energetically nonetheless. As the banker studied the letter, however, Sam noticed his features tightening.

"Three livres and twelve sols," Grimaldi murmured in a confident tone. "Yes, yes, that's perfect. I'll go get you that."

He stood up from his chair and entered the building behind him.

"Don't move," he added. "I'm going to bring you the money."

Sam saw him disappear through the door. Then his shadow appeared on one of the bank's windows: Grimaldi was waving his arms as if he were calling his servants. Two shapes appeared at his side, and he seemed to be giving them orders. *Uh-oh!* thought Sam. *This is about me.* If Melchior had told Mr. Klugg that his coat had been stolen with the note inside, then Mr. Klugg might have told the banker in turn. If so, Grimaldi would surely alert the watch. And this was no time for that — it was never a good time for that!

Before someone could come out and yell, "Stop, thief!" Sam moved swiftly away under the awnings. When he reached the edge of the square, he began to run, losing himself in the crowd as he headed toward the graveyard.

The coins didn't work. *The coins didn't work!* He tried turning them every which way, but the stone statue remained unmoved. The coins were the right size, even if their edges were irregular. But nothing happened: no sign of warmth, not the slightest vibration. The stone was as cold and dead as all the others in the cemetery! In a rage, Sam threw the coins into a ditch. He was stuck in Bruges!

Needless to say, the evening was pretty gloomy. Yser asked him how he had spent the long afternoon, but Sam only answered with vague references to his need to earn money. As for Baltus, he was more excited than ever — first at the idea of showing his painting the next day, then because he thought he was on the verge of discovering Van Eyck's secret.

"I'm very close, I can feel it! The oil is still too viscous to mix with the color, but only a tiny bit is needed! The guild will soon elect me first master!"

He had apparently forgotten Sam's role in his spectacular progress. To top it all off, the maid was as unfriendly as ever, serving Sam half the amount of rich bouillon as the others, and giving him a bare bone disguised as meat. He wasn't hungry anyway.

Long past midnight, Sam lay stretched out on his bed, eyes wide open. He had thought he'd been clever with the money-changing business, but instead he had wasted precious time. Where should he be looking now? The cemetery chapel was sealed shut, and he hadn't found anything in searching the Vieux-Bois cemetery itself. So where was the coin? And what about his father? How could he save his father if he wasn't able to save himself?

His only satisfaction was the photographs. Not those of the tournament, which were out of focus and badly framed — the knights looked as if they were wearing cheap Halloween costumes. But the scenes of Bruges he had shot while walking to the cemetery — the walls, the bell tower, the steeples, the panorama of the city — they were something, anyway.

He heard a faint creaking in the hallway. It was the front door again! This time Sam wasn't in the least sleepy. He dressed quickly and tiptoed out of the studio. The key had been turned and the lock opened. Outside, the snow of recent days had given way to a thin layer of blackish mud. Footsteps led off toward the right. Sam stepped into the street as he finished buttoning his coat.

The mysterious stroller seemed to be heading toward the

canal. Sam fell into step behind him. After crossing three or four alleys, he reached the bridge across the Reie River. There was nobody in sight.

He suddenly felt himself grabbed from behind. "So here he is, the dirty little sneak!"

Someone seized his arm, spinning him around. A tall young man with blond hair faced him, scowling. "I knew you were in on it! Baltus has been taken for a ride!"

Behind the young man's broad shoulders, Sam could see a young woman with a hood over her head. Yser!

"You were following her, weren't you?"

"No," answered Sam, trying to free himself. "I didn't know it was her! This is the third time somebody has gone out of the house at night, and . . ."

"You were following her! Just as you're part of the gang that attacked them! I'll beat you black and blue!"

"Wait, Friedrich!" Yser broke in. "We can't be sure he's lying. It may just be a coincidence."

"A coincidence? He shows up out of nowhere, like that, just to help you? And he winds up making himself at home? He's one of the constable's spies, I tell you! What he deserves is a good beating!"

"Not so loud, Friedrich, for the love of heaven! If my father learns that . . ."

"I can shout if you like," Sam said. "Then we can find out what the neighbors think."

"Let him go, Friedrich," said Yser. "It won't do to wake the neighborhood."

Reluctantly the young man freed him.

"You should have told me you thought I was a spy," said

Sam. "I told you yesterday, the constable is no friend of mine! He thinks I'm one of those robbers too!"

"That would surprise me," grumbled Friedrich. "He's the one who sent them."

"He sent them?"

"Friedrich is sure of it," said Yser. "From the very beginning, he's been convinced that the constable hired them to attack us."

"To attack you? When he hopes to marry you?"

"He's devious," Friedrich hissed. "He wanted to break Baltus's arm so he couldn't paint anymore. No painting, no prize in the contest."

"And no prize in the contest increases his chances of marrying me," added Yser. "He knows very well that my father favors this marriage mainly because he doesn't want me to lack for anything. If money were coming into the house again, my father might hesitate."

So the constable had set an ambush for Baltus to keep him from winning the contest. That's why he was so annoyed at Sam's presence! Sam was the intruder who had spoiled everything.

"Yser can't marry him," Friedrich said, putting an arm around her. "His doings aren't very Christian. I've gone into his laboratory a few times, and he practices magic in there! It's full of strange powders, old books, even dead animals in jars. I can't see Yser living there, it would drive her mad."

"You can get into his laboratory?"

"I'm a valet at the Prinsenhof, where he lives. I sometimes wait on him in the tower. When he works on his stupid medals, believe me, there's enough smoke to make you think the place is on fire!"

"That's where we met, at the Prinsenhof," said Yser. "Since then we've been in love."

Sam had guessed as much.

"And you see each other at night?"

"My father won't hear of us getting married. Friedrich may not have a fortune," she added bitterly, "but he is honest and brave. Completely the opposite of that pretentious Klugg!"

"Klugg?" said Sam, startled. "The constable's name is Klugg?"

"Of course, why?"

"Klugg! But . . . In that case, you're right! He's the one! It's the constable! He paid the robbers. I have proof!"

Friedrich looked at Sam as if he'd lost his mind. "Are you making fun of us?"

"Yser, remember! The coat I took from the robber the other afternoon, it had a pocket on the inside with a bearer note signed Klugg — Klugg, as in the constable! It promised three livres and twelve sols against execution of a certain mission. And that mission was to attack your father!"

"The dirty rat!" shouted the valet angrily. "He deserves to . . ."

"Not so loud, Friedrich, please! And what about this note?" Yser asked Sam hopefully. "Did you keep it? Showing it to my father will open his eyes!"

"I gave it to Grimaldi, the banker," Sam admitted. "I had no way of knowing how important it was!"

An embarrassed silence followed. The two lovers whispered urgently as Sam thought over the situation.

"I have an idea," he began.

Things were gradually becoming clear in his mind. If Klugg was behind this affair, maybe he'd also been in the wood, watching to be sure that his plan was carried out correctly. If

Sam's theory was right, the coin had to be close to the statue at the time Sam arrived for him to be able to use it to leave. Did Klugg have the coin with him that day?

"He works with metal, doesn't he?" Sam continued. "I saw the candleholder that he made for you. Do you know if he ever makes coins?"

"Coins, no; that's forbidden," said Friedrich. "On the other hand, I've seen all sorts of plates in his laboratory, medals and lots of other things."

Medals . . .

"What is your idea?" asked Yser.

"You need evidence against the constable to stop the marriage, right? I'll get it right from his laboratory, if Friedrich will lead me there."

CHAPTER SIXTEEN

The Alchemist

"Pssst!"

Sam turned around. Friedrich was standing in the doorway at the far end of the room, gesturing for him to come. None of the three hundred invited guests in the immense vaulted hall of the Prinsenhof paid any attention. The thirty-odd portraits in the competition were arranged along the walls, but most of the guests had clustered in front of a big table where servants in gray and white — the count's colors — served hot spiced wine. A murmur went through the assemblage as Philip the Good made a majestic entrance, wearing a gleaming red coat and surrounded by his advisors. The constable moved forward to greet the count. Sam kept his back toward him, pretending to be admiring the paintings as he gradually worked his way to the door.

"Dear friends," said the count amiably, "welcome to the Prinsenhof! I am sure that the painters of Bruges have done wonders. So let us see these portraits, and may the contest begin!"

Amid the acclamations, Sam slipped out.

"They'll be busy for a good long time," Friedrich whispered. "Come on!"

They took a series of passageways reserved for servants to the tower at the corner of the palace.

"These are the constable's lodgings," explained Friedrich. "The stairway down leads to the kitchens, the one up leads to the apartments and the laboratory."

"Is there any danger of running into someone?"

"Everybody is busy with the reception, even the constable."

"How do I get into the laboratory?"

Friedrich held up an iron ring with a large key on it.

"Perfect," said Sam approvingly. "You better stay here to warn me in case anyone comes."

"Don't you want me to come with you?"

"If they catch both of us, you'll have even less chance to marry Yser! It's safer for you to be the lookout. Is there a place where I can hide if things go wrong?"

"The floor above the laboratory, at the top of the tower."

"All right. If someone comes, you run and warn me, and we'll hide up there. With a little luck, no one will notice us."

"How are you going to get the evidence?"

"I'll find it, don't worry. There's something I'm looking for too."

Sam headed up the stairs. On the second landing he turned the key in the large lock, which was shaped like a wolf's mouth. The door creaked on its hinges as he pushed it open. The light from two wide windows revealed a circular room — as one would expect of a tower — crammed with an incredible jumble of books, bottles, tables laden with parchments, stuffed birds, and strange engravings. Metal instruments hung from the ceiling like rusty sausages, and a burned smell pervaded everything, just as in Baltus's studio. Just in front of the fireplace stood the furnace where Klugg probably conducted his experiments. The shelves held a small still to refine alcohol, pots filled with herbs and powders, and jars containing small dead animals; some were dried mice and lizards, while others floated in a greenish liquid. Sam tried to recall what little he knew about alchemy. He had heard talk of potions thanks to Harry Potter, and of making gold from lead or mercury, he couldn't quite remember which; and that was about it. He would have to go on instinct.

He walked over to the brick furnace, which stood waist-high and gave off a gentle warmth. The lower compartment held glowing coals. Above it rested an oval basin half covered with warm ashes. Was that how one made gold? There didn't seem to be any of it in the laboratory. Sam opened a big chest under the first window and found the stock of plates and medals that Friedrich had mentioned. Apparently these were original, more or less finished creations, and represented Klugg's efforts in metallurgy. Sam even recognized the twisted branches that must have served as a model for Yser's candlestick. But no coins.

He headed for the desk near the second window, and his pulse suddenly started to race: A whole stack of sketches of the stone statue had been casually tossed on top of the books! They were charcoal sketches, in particular of the Vieux-Bois tomb seen from different angles. One of the parchments showed the sun with its six rays, surrounded by numbers listing angles and lengths. It was a scale drawing with precise measurements! The constable was clearly trying to discover the statue's secret!

Trembling, Sam walked around the desk. He sat down in the chair facing the open book on which Klugg must have been working. The pages were covered with incomprehensible symbols, but also with little drawings of a half-dozen stone statues in different settings: a temple that could be Greek, a tree stump, a rock on a hillside, the base of a statue like those on Easter Island. . . . It was almost a catalog of stone statues! Sam took a deep breath and tried to keep his thoughts straight. His eyes ran over the sheet in front of him, where some words had been written in capital letters. He guessed that it was a Latin translation of one of the passages in the old book of spells:

SI QUIS SEPTEM CALCULOS COLLEGERIT, SOLIS POTIETUR.

SI EFFECERIT UT SEX RADII FULGEANT,

COR EJUS TEMPUS RESOLVET.

TUM PERPETUUM AESTUM COGNOSCET.

The red ink was still damp, a sign that the constable had left his work to join the reception. Sam cursed his inner simultaneous translator, which at the moment didn't allow him to understand anything other than the language of Bruges. He should have followed Lily's example and studied Latin! The text might be important. He took the paper and stuffed it under his jacket, thinking he would examine it later. He then turned the pages of the old book of spells. It didn't deal only with the stone statue, but also with monsters and unfamiliar objects that must be involved in the magic rituals of the time. Or at least that's what he guessed from the illustrations: a bat with a child's face, a stuffed bird beating its wings, a furnace like the one in the laboratory, a gnarled staff encrusted with precious stones . . .

"Instructive, isn't it?"

Sam spun around and found himself nose to nose with the constable, who was holding a dagger. Oddly enough, the man didn't seem angry; on the contrary, he looked rather pleased.

"I wondered why you had left the great hall, my boy. Or, rather, no, I didn't wonder." He pointed to a pivoting wooden panel under one of the shelves, revealing a hidden passage. "The Prinsenhof has its little secrets, just as you do. You know how to operate the sun, don't you? Was it thanks to the sun that you appeared the other day to defend Baltus?"

Sam was unable to answer.

"And it was you who went to the banker Grimaldi yesterday? I know it; he described your ugly face. You planned to get the three livres, yes?" Klugg drew a piece of paper from his doublet and waved it under Sam's nose. "You recognize the note, I suppose? Too bad that old snake Grimaldi didn't catch you right away, it would have saved me . . ."

He left the sentence uncompleted, as if not to alarm his prey, but his nostrils were trembling strangely, and Sam didn't like the yellow gleam in his eye.

"Do you know how long I've been interested in the sun?"

Sam shrugged to show his ignorance.

"More than a year ago, I was told about this strange carving in the Vieux-Bois cemetery, on an ancient grave said to be older than the cemetery itself. You know what legends are like. As it turned out, the day I went there was the burial of Baltus's wife. That's when I met Yser for the first time. Two suns in the same location couldn't have been a coincidence."

With his free hand, he absentmindedly turned the pages

of the book of spells. "Do you know the origin of the word 'alchemy,' my boy? No, obviously not. It's *shemesh*, the Hebrew word for 'sun.' We get everything from the sun. Everything! Heat, light, life. By attaining the purity of the sun's fire, the alchemist can transform metal into gold. That's what all the books say. Some of them also speak of the superior powers of the 'sun on the stone' — *The Treatise on the Thirteen Virtues of Magic,* for example, which I bought from an Arab. A difficult book, but full of useful lessons. For weeks I've been trying to solve its riddles, in particular its method of melting coins. I hope you will help me."

Klugg moved his blade under Sam's chin.

"Hel — help you?" Sam said. "How could I help you? I can't understand any of this writing and . . ."

"Tut-tut! I know that you have made the sun work, my boy. The stone was warm after your passage. I have tried again and again to put my coin inside the stone, but it refuses to change into gold. I suppose it lacks the necessary heat. But you . . . you can create that heat, can't you?"

The point of the knife stung Sam's Adam's apple, and a small drop of blood rolled down his neck.

"Think carefully, my boy. You have absconded with a bearer note and tried to have yourself paid by the banker Grimaldi. Then you broke into my laboratory in hopes of stealing heaven knows what. No one would blame me for trying to arrest you, or for your death if the arrest ended badly. So you'd do well to answer me. Yes or no, did you use the sun on the stone in the Vieux-Bois cemetery?"

Sam had no choice. "I . . . yes."

The constable breathed more deeply, and the knife trembled slightly. "Good," he sighed. "You're a good boy. And now . . ."

There were three loud knocks on the door.

"Master! Master!" It was Friedrich's voice.

"Who is it?" roared the constable.

"It's Van Todds, master! You must come right away!"

Van Todds? wondered Sam.

"What is it?"

"The count has been attacked! He is calling for you!"

The constable hesitated for a fraction of a second. "Come in!"

Friedrich opened the door and turned pale when he saw the knife in the constable's hand. "Master, what . . ."

"Listen to me, Van Todds. I've just surprised this trouble-maker searching my laboratory. I want you to keep him here until I come back. He must not speak to anyone! Do you understand?"

Friedrich agreed, but he was visibly troubled.

"And now tell me what happened."

"A — a guest," stammered Friedrich. "He pulled a dagger while the count was admiring the paintings."

"Is the count wounded?"

"Yes, in the arm. He sent me to look for you."

"And the attacker?"

"Is being pursued."

"All right. You're going to take this knife, Van Todds, and watch this boy until I return. If you do exactly what I tell you, there will be a rich reward for you."

Friedrich took the knife while avoiding looking at Sam. The constable observed the scene for a moment, then started for the door. He hadn't taken more than three steps before Friedrich grabbed a flat-bottomed pan hanging from the ceiling and gave his master a terrific blow on the head. Klugg crumpled to the floor without a word.

"I've wanted to do that for quite a while," Friedrich said soberly. He kicked the door shut and turned to Sam, who hadn't budged. "Are you all right? It seemed to be taking you a long time, and I came up to see what had happened. When I heard voices . . ."

"The count? Was he really attacked?"

"No, of course not. I had to make something up! But there was no way I could let the constable leave. Do you have the evidence?"

"Your . . . your last name is Van Todds, is that right?"

The young man smiled. "Yes. And so?"

"I'm going to give you your evidence. And in exchange you're going to make me a promise: to marry Yser."

"That's a wonderful promise, my friend! That marriage is all I want! Except that after what's happened, Klugg here won't send us any flowers!"

"All you have to do is leave town for a while. You could even take Yser with you. I'm sure you'll manage. The important thing is for you to get married. Here, take this paper. It should convince Baltus."

Sam showed him the bearer note on the desk and watched while he read it. Friedrich Van Todds! He was Alicia Todds's great-great-great-great-something-grandfather! As long as he married Yser and had children, that is. That was why Yser and Alicia had such a family resemblance!

"What a pig this Klugg is!" exclaimed Friedrich.

"We better not hang around," said Sam. "He could wake up at any moment. What's the quickest way out?"

"Downstairs through the kitchens. But first I have to give this note to Baltus and tell Yser what happened. Otherwise the constable will find a way to blame me for everything. As for you, do you have what you wanted?"

"Almost."

Sam bent over the constable and patted the trousers under his doublet, where he discovered a small purse knotted shut at the belt. He slipped two fingers inside: It contained a round coin with a hole in the middle.

"I have to leave, Friedrich," he said, trying to hide his emotion. "I am very, very happy to have known you and Yser. More than you can imagine."

"Come on, Waagen, don't look like that. We'll all see one another again — maybe at Malines, eh? That would be a good place to hide, wouldn't it?"

"Yes, a good place," whispered Sam.

They shook hands and went downstairs in silence. Friedrich took the hallway that led to the reception hall while Sam continued on toward the kitchens. He was torn between impatience to return to his own time and the feeling that he was forever abandoning a part of his history, and deserting Friedrich and Yser in the process.

Maybe that was the price of the trip.

CHAPTER SEVENTEEN

Latin Translation

Sam stood up unsteadily. He was in complete darkness, but the smells were familiar: old books, curtains, dust . . . He was back in Faulkner's Antique Books! He felt a rush of gratitude for Lily, who must have been thinking about him, though she wasn't here now. He retrieved the cell phone from the cavity, congratulating himself on cleverly bringing back proof of his adventures, and turned it on: FRIDAY, JUNE 11, 4:42 P.M. A day of absence all told, and a few problems ahead, but nothing compared with what his father was suffering in Vlad Tepes's castle — unless Allan had returned in the meantime.

Sam left the hidden room with the same seasick sensation as last time; it felt as if the house were swaying on its foundations. He went up to the kitchen and ran himself a tall glass of water. There weren't any cookies in the cabinets, so he had to settle for the disgusting remains of some old crackers. He switched on the television near the microwave. He must have still been under the effects of his "transfer," because the man narrating a documentary about lions in the savannah was repeating each sentence:

"Tabitha is the most playful of the litter —

"Tabitha is the most playful of the litter, while Paulus is the boldest —

"While Paulus is the boldest. As soon as his mother turns her back, he's the one —

"As soon as his mother turns her back, he's the one who leads his brothers and sisters to discover the wide world —

"Who leads his brothers and sisters to discover the wide world."

Sam watched the screen in a daze. Tabitha, Paulus: Mother lions had strange taste in names. Paulus swatted a poor passing beetle twice, who then rolled over and over twice. This déjà vu effect was especially unnerving because it hadn't happened at any of the locations Sam had visited in time; it was only happening now, in the present. Fortunately, the echo began to subside after ten minutes or so.

Feeling a little more alert, Sam realized two things: One, he really didn't smell very good — he hadn't felt like using the trough of icy water in Baltus's bathroom; and two, he had some odd scarlet stains on his shirt. He pulled it off over his head and quickly realized what had happened. He had slipped the constable's parchment under his coat, and the red ink must have stained the white cloth. When he had reached the Vieux-Bois cemetery, he had put the coin on the sun without paying attention to his clothes. The coat and the jacket had vanished during the trip, as had the paper hidden beneath them — perhaps from the heat, or the energy given off by the statue. In any case, the text from the old book of spells was now *printed* on his shirt, even if it was printed backward.

Sam ran upstairs to his bedroom and grabbed a piece of

paper and a pencil. He then pressed the shirt against the window and copied the text:

SI QUIS SEPTEM CALCULOS COLLEGERIT, SOLIS POTIETUR.
SI EFFECERIT UT SEX RADII FULGEANT,
COR EJUS TEMPUS RESOLVET.
TUM PERPETUUM AESTUM COGNOSCET.

To be honest, even written on twenty-first-century graph paper with a twenty-first-century pencil, the sentences didn't tell him much. Lily would probably be more inspired. He chose clean clothes from his closet and decided to take a shower. He thought he looked different in the bathroom mirror. Weren't his shoulders wider? And his thighs stronger? And wasn't there a little more fuzz on his cheeks? Unless the fact that he was tired was making him look older.

Once he was clean and dry, Sam zipped up his bag and got ready to head to Grandma's. He was wondering what to tell her when he heard the scraping of a chair in the kitchen. Had Paulus and Tabitha tumbled out of the TV while hunting for the beetle? Silently Sam went downstairs.

Standing in front of the open refrigerator was another kind of dangerous animal, in an elegant cream-colored suit and tanned face: Rudolf, Aunt Evelyn's knight in shining armor.

"Would you like a beer?" Sam said as cheerfully as possible.

Rudolf turned to him, his jaw clenched. "You little jerk!" he thundered. "Is this where you've been hiding?" He slammed the refrigerator door shut. In his right hand he held the cell phone Sam had left on the table.

"You think it's funny playing us for suckers, eh? Do you know what state your grandparents are in? And your aunt?"

When Rudolf raised his hand to strike him, Sam didn't blink. But at the last moment, the man changed his mind and simply grabbed him by the arm. "What have you been doing since yesterday? We've been looking for you everywhere!"

"I've been here at home," answered Sam. "This is my home, isn't it?"

"As long as your father is gone, you are your family's responsibility! You must obey us!"

"You aren't my family!"

A murderous gleam flickered in Rudolf's eyes. "We'll see about that!" he shouted. "And what about this phone? Lily thought she'd lost it, but you stole it from her, of course! What for? To sell it? I bet you're one of those street junkies, ready to do anything to pay for your drugs!"

Sam was tempted to tell him that Lily alone had given him her cell phone — without asking him, moreover. But that would only have gotten his cousin into trouble.

"You can see that I didn't sell it, since it's here!"

"I ought to take you to the police. That would cure you of your need to lie. Wannabe delinquents like you, if you don't break them right at the beginning . . . You're lucky you have your aunt to keep you in line!"

Without releasing Sam's arm, Rudolf dragged him to the car. Sam barely resisted; he didn't feel like taking the bus back to his grandparents' house anyway. On the other hand, he had to undergo a stiff interrogation during the trip, spiced with a few cutting remarks about his father's irresponsibility in leaving him on his own. Sam bit his lip and forcefully reminded himself of the virtues of silence.

Once at Grandma's, his would-be uncle metamorphosed from aggressive bulldog into protective sheepdog, bringing the lost lamb back to the fold. "I found him, Mrs. Faulkner, and it wasn't easy! He claims that he slept at the Barenboim Street house, but I'm not sure we can believe him."

Grandma rushed over to Sam and covered him with kisses. "Sammy! My Sammy! I was so frightened, so frightened! Tell me what happened!"

"I needed to be alone, Grandma. I'm allowed to spend a little time in my own home, aren't I?"

"Of course, of course! But why run away like that without saying a word?"

"If you want my opinion," Rudolf said sarcastically, "he didn't want to be around to get his report card."

Ouch! The report card; Sam hadn't thought of that.

"We got it this morning. It's true that it isn't very good," Grandpa admitted, "but you haven't had an easy time of it these days. Besides, it's not the end of the world!"

"I still think you should send him to a boarding school next year," Rudolf said. "If Allan doesn't come back, you may have to."

There was a painful silence.

"He will come back," Sam said in a strong voice. "I promise he'll come back!"

Grandpa nodded. "Of course he'll come back! Allan always comes back! Oh, by the way, Sammy, one of your friends telephoned. Onk or Monk; I didn't quite get it."

"What did he want?"

"To remind you about your judo tournament tomorrow. He seemed to really want you to be there."

Of course; Monk was looking forward to tearing him to pieces in front of everybody!

"You know, I'm not in very good shape," said Sam apologetically. "I haven't really trained this week, so if I'm just going to get eliminated in the first round . . ."

His grandmother smiled indulgently and patted his arm, but Rudolf wouldn't hear of it.

"If you give in to him on this, Mrs. Faulkner, you won't be doing him any favors. Samuel needs rules, discipline. And competition is the best way to forge his character. If he gives up at the first obstacle, how will he manage later?"

What business was it of this suit-wearing idiot's? Unfortunately, Grandma seemed swayed by his argument.

"You usually like judo, don't you?" she said to Sam.

"Yes, it's just that I'm a little tired and . . ."

"I think Allan would have wanted you to go," cut in Grandpa.

Rudolf clinched his revenge with barely restrained glee. "We could all go, to encourage him! At least then we would know where he was."

Sam was sent to his room for the evening and forbidden to talk to Lily as punishment for his "theft" of the cell phone. He was allowed to come down only for dinner, where he underwent a second barrage of insults from Aunt Evelyn: "dropout," "quasi-delinquent," "future bum," and other cheerful predictions. His future seemed to be taking shape: If his father didn't reappear, he would be sent to the Meriadek boarding school in the United States. Once again, Sam thought it wisest to keep quiet, though he did manage to give Lily a few significant looks.

When he was back in his bedroom, Sam took four or five sheets of scratch paper, wrote a few words on each, and crumpled them. He then stepped out onto the balcony and threw the paper balls through Lily's open window. She was still downstairs with her mother, but she would come up sooner or later, and she would find the papers on her carpet and contact him.

In the meantime, Sam sat down at his computer. He searched for "Hans Baltus" on the Internet without success: There were indeed a few Hans Baltuses, including a musician and a bicycle racer, but none had any connection with the medieval painter. He learned in passing that a Klugg or Klug was a kind of rum cake, that the Yser was a river in the region of Bruges, and that Bruges itself was located in northwest Europe, as he had guessed, in modern-day Belgium. He then skimmed through virtual art galleries of Flemish painting, but again with no success: Van Eyck's paintings were often mentioned, but there was no sign of a portrait of Yser. The white hands and black dress he had painted hadn't survived through the ages . . .

After a while, a little jingle alerted him that Lily had sent an instant message to the screen name Sam indicated in his papers. Her screen name: *boyonthebeach.*

boyonthebeach: My room = garbage dump! Thanx a lot! JK. I'm really glad 2 talk 2 U. Everything iz going crazy here! I don't know watz wrong with my mother, it must B Rudolf. How R U? U looked K.O. at dinner.

stormskater: I didn't find my father = not the right time. Did U get the coins?

boyonthebeach: I saw it in the Book of Time. U were in Bruges, 1430, rite? The coins R OK in my bag. I didnt ever stop thinkin bout U!

stormskater: 1000 thank U's. Without U I would have gotten killed! I'll tell U later. How iz yr Latin? I want U 2 translate something. It might be important: "SI QUIS SEPTEM CALCULOS COLLEGERIT, SOLIS POTIETUR. SI EFFECERIT UT SEX RADII FULGEANT, COR EJUS TEMPUS RESOLVET. TUM PERPETUUM AESTUM COGNOSCET." I understand 0! Thanx!!!

Lily promised to do it as quickly as possible, and even to call the special Latin tutor her mother had found if she got stuck. Sam stretched out on his bed. He was on the verge of falling asleep when someone knocked gently at his door.

"Sammy, can I come in?"

"Of course, Grandma."

She closed the door carefully, as if she didn't want anyone to see her. "Don't think I enjoyed sending you to your room," she whispered. "But because you won't explain what's going on — the cell phone, the disappearances — your grandfather and I can't stand by and do nothing!"

"I'm not criticizing you for anything, Grandma."

"I know," she said as she sat down on the quilt. "That's just what worries me. But I didn't come up here to lecture you. You got enough of that from Evelyn! No, I wanted to tell you something important, though I don't know if this will cheer you up. Grandpa told you about Allan's internship a few years ago, didn't he? He must have said how upset I was."

Sam nodded. "You were scared something had happened to him, right? But you couldn't leave the grocery store to go to Egypt."

"We would have done it if it had been necessary. But in a sense it wasn't, really. How can I put this? I was far away, thousands of miles away, and I clearly sensed that Allan was in danger. And yet I swear, Sammy, I was *absolutely* sure he wasn't dead. When I was asleep at night, I sometimes had very short flashes . . . I'd be lying if I said that I saw him. I mainly *felt* his presence. It's something a mother doesn't mistake, even in dreams. He was there, surrounded by fog, among all these strange shapes, like a movie set. Sometimes he was smiling, other times he looked unhappy."

She was shaking, and Sam sat up and put his arms around her. "I believe you, Grandma."

"You're sweet, Sammy. But that's not all," she said, starting to sob. "The day . . . the day your mother went off the road on the hill . . . You were at the hospital, remember?"

Sam remembered every moment of that terrible day. He had just had his appendix removed, and a nurse came to tell him about the accident. Her name was Belinda. She was a redhead, with her hair up in a bun, and had large, somewhat stupid-looking dark eyes. The panicky expression on her face was forever stamped in his memory.

"When the policeman phoned the house, I knew there was no hope. He told us that she was being brought to the emergency room, but for me there was no doubt left. I *felt* that too."

Sam didn't want to relive it.

"And now, Grandma? What do you *feel* about Dad?"

She looked him right in the eyes, and tears were shining on her cheeks. "He is alive, darling, I'm sure of it. Trust your old grandmother. He's alive!"

"And is he smiling or frowning?"

"The fog in my dreams is too thick these days; I can't make out anything. But he's there, I'm sure of it. So please, Sammy, don't do anything too — hasty, or dangerous . . . I don't want him to have anything to reproach us with when he comes back."

She kissed him on the forehead and tiptoed away. Sam lay on his bed for a moment, turning what he had heard over and over in every direction. Should he believe Grandma? They had studied premonitions and other extrasensory perception in science once. Mr. Maverick felt that people who claimed to have these kinds of premonitory experiences were just using their memory selectively: "If I tell myself ten times that a blue car is going to come around the corner," he explained, "and on the tenth time a blue car finally appears, I'll forget my initial failures and only remember my success. Does that mean I can predict the future? Am I given to premonitions? No, of course not. But it's comforting for us to think we can master things beyond our control."

A week earlier, Sam would have applied that line of reasoning without hesitation. His grandmother was interpreting after the fact and to her advantage events that were subject to complete chance. But his point of view on many things had changed in the last week. His days of certainty were long gone!

As he thought about it, Sam could occasionally hear bits

of muffled conversation on the other side of the wall. Lily was working at translating his text. Tired of waiting, he wound up falling asleep.

A jingle from the computer woke him up around one o'clock. He rushed to the screen: it was a message from *boyonthebeach*.

> boyonthebeach: Thanks 4 the vacation HW! I had trouble n finally the Latin teacher helped me by e-mail. Good thing she likes me! Here iz the translation from her:
> "HE WHO GATHERS THE SEVEN TOKENS WILL BE THE MASTER OF THE SUN. IF HE CAN MAKE THE SIX RAYS SHINE, ITS HEART WILL BE THE KEY TO TIME. HE WILL THEN KNOW THE IMMORTAL HEAT."

Sam read and reread the message a dozen times, trying to figure out what it meant. *The seven tokens; master of the sun; make the six rays shine; the immortal heat.* Of course that had a direct connection with the stone statue. But some of the expressions weren't very clear, and he understood why Klugg must have thought that by putting a coin in the cavity he would succeed in changing it into gold. But alchemy wasn't involved here, only "traveling." *Its heart will be the key to time!*

> stormskater: U R the most incredible cousin in the galaxy!!! OK here is how I C the text. In my opinion: tokens = coins. U have 2 get 7 coins with holes in them 2 really make the statue work (= choose your time?). The 6 rays R those of the sun. How 2 make them shine? No idea. The sun must light up, maybe? The immortal heat, thatz the feeling of burning that I told U about: U

burn but U dont die = heat + immortal. Well I guess. Tell me if
thatz right according to U!

He waited a few minutes, hoping that *boyonthebeach* would
confirm his guesses, but after fifteen minutes, he had to face
the fact: *boyonthebeach* was probably sound asleep.

CHAPTER EIGHTEEN

Surprise

There wasn't a single space left in the gymnasium parking lot when the Faulkners arrived at the judo tournament. Rudolf had to park his brand-new Porsche 4×4 a hundred yards away, behind a run-down building — a small satisfaction for Sam. Grandma had put on her pretty flowered dress, which made her look more cheerful than her face showed, while Grandpa reminisced about his grocery-store days, including such fascinating topics as the best-selling brands of American canned goods. Sam himself hadn't opened his mouth once, so everyone would know that he was being dragged to the slaughter by force — which was exactly the case. Aunt Evelyn hadn't deigned to come; she thought hockey was better for building character and had told Allan so a thousand times. And Lily had simply not been invited, on the principle of keeping her away from her cousin's bad influence.

Lily told Sam in an e-mail that she had asked for a ton of books to be put aside at the town library, and that she had to go there in any case. Given the bloodbath he expected in the tournament, Sam was just as glad she wasn't along.

When he entered the gym, his first impulse was to find Monk. The stands were already half full of spectators talking noisily, and their voices echoed on the metal ceiling. Spotlights lit the half-dozen tatami mats as the referees checked to see that they were set up properly. Team captains talked among themselves, a few judokas in track suits punched and kicked the air, competitors consulted the match brackets on the computers — but there was no sign of Monk. Was it a lightning sore throat? A sprained wrist from lifting too many sandwiches? Or maybe a sudden attack of conscience in which he realized it was wrong to smash his schoolmates' teeth in? One could always dream. . . .

Sam left his family on the Nicholas Gill bleachers — named for the great Canadian judo champion — and shuffled listlessly toward the locker room. He promptly ran into Master Yuko, who greeted him with a slight smile. The sensei was hardly talkative, but he took a great interest in his students and often knew more about them than their parents did — profoundly human qualities that accounted for the success of his teaching.

"I'm glad you're here, Sam. I know you aren't too fired up about this tournament, but it will be a good experience for you. Don't be afraid to trust yourself, all right? Now go change, and be sure to do your stretching."

Sam muttered a thank-you. He chose a locker off to one side and slowly undressed, ignoring his friends' jokes about the competition. He was one of the youngest competitors there — he had been fourteen for only a week — so his chances of doing well in the tournament hovered somewhere around absolute zero. He pulled on his uniform — his *judogi*, technically — and his brand-new brown belt, and did a few stretches and bends. Then he went back to the arena.

The audience's noise level had grown louder as the stands filled and the sixty-odd competitors lined up in front of the judges. Monk was indeed there, a mountain of muscles and aggressiveness. Luckily he didn't see Sam arrive, occupied as he was in teasing one of his potential rivals, a tall, slim blond boy. Sam immediately went to the other end of the line and kept his head down.

The loudspeakers blared some lively folk music, and the announcer officially launched the Twenty-seventh Annual Sainte-Mary–Fontana judo tournament. The two towns, Sainte-Mary and Fontana, had been rivals since their founding, and for the first 150 years of their existence, their young people fought "mêlées" that were as violent as they were spectacular. After World War II, the enmity subsided; but the tradition inspired the judo clubs to organize all-category matchups for eleven- to thirteen-year-olds and fourteen- to sixteen-year-olds. The winner of each was considered the regional champion.

Because the Sainte-Mary team was so much bigger than the Fontana squad, it had long been decided to pair off competitors without respect for their town of origin, which explained why Sam risked facing Monk again. The preceding year, Sam had fallen — in every sense of the word — to the unsinkable Monk. Though Monk was only a few months older than Sam, he'd flipped him like a pancake in forty-three seconds flat. He went on to win the eleven- to thirteen-year-olds trophy, and this year he no doubt planned to take the fourteen- to sixteen-year-olds prize. Who could stop him? He wasn't the oldest competitor, but he was certainly the strongest and, in any case, the most vicious. Everybody prayed not to have him in their bracket.

Sam headed for the tatami marked for his initial contest. He glanced toward the stands, where Grandma waved encouragement, then took the red belt the referee handed him and tied it over his own, so the spectators could more easily distinguish him from his opponent. He was facing Pete Moret, one of his friends from the club, and Sam bowed to him as they took their places on the mat. If he truly wanted this to be over quickly, he could fall to the mat as soon as the referee started the match, but he didn't want to give Rudolf the satisfaction. Besides, Pete was hardly one of the team's aces, and Master Yuko would probably find Sam's defeat suspicious.

"Hajime!" the referee said. Sam took two steps forward and seized the collar of Moret's *gi.* He knew Pete would try his signature move, a hip throw that he used in every one of his matches, and he let Pete tire himself out trying to place it. Then, on his first opportunity, Sam crisply swept away Pete's support leg and threw him on his back. The referee announced: *"Waza-ari!"*

Waza-ari meant seven points for Sam, an excellent beginning.

On the ground, Sam followed up with one of his favorite holds, where his right arm pressed down on Pete's neck while his left arm and body weight pinned him to the mat. He needed to hold Pete for twenty-five seconds to score a pin: "Twenty-two, twenty-three, twenty-four . . ."

"Ippon!" announced the referee.

Ippon meant ten points — and instant victory! Sam had won. Sam and Pete stood up, adjusted their *gi*s, and bowed to each other. The referee pointed to Sam to indicate his triumph. Grandma and Grandpa applauded frantically in the stands.

As he put on his sandals to go back to the locker room, he heard Monk murmur behind him. "Not bad, Faulkner. Pete Moret's pretty much your level. I wouldn't have wanted you to lose, if you know what I mean."

"I'm happy not to disappoint you," Sam said without turning around. Then he took off, preferring not to think of their possible bout.

The rest of the morning went by like a dream. Every opponent was someone he could handle, often a teammate whom he had beaten at least once in the past. Sam had always been a pretty good judoka, at least where speed and technique were concerned, but for some reason he felt stronger and more comfortable than ever before. Looking at his reflection in the bathroom mirror, he wound up deciding that he *had* put on some muscles. Was it the time spent in the crane at Bruges? Maybe time travel was as good as weight lifting!

He approached his fourth match of the morning with confidence. His opponent this time was a Fontana boy, a quick and speedy brown belt he didn't know. As soon as the referee stepped back, the boy caught Sam by surprise by knocking his right foot out from under him. He fell on his side and curled into a ball to avoid being pinned, but the boy still earned a *yuko* — five points — for his clever move. Neither of the two was able to get the advantage on the ground, so the referee separated them — *"Matte!"* — and the fight resumed with them standing up.

It was only in the last minute that Sam glimpsed a solution, thanks to a somewhat unorthodox *uki otoshi*. His adversary had incautiously advanced, so Sam knelt to tip him forward, then abruptly shoved him back. Twice unbalanced, the Fontana boy fell on his back, which earned Sam a beautiful *waza-ari!* When time was called, Sam won, if just barely, with seven points to his opponent's five.

When they met at noon in the cafeteria near the gymnasium, Grandma was delighted. "The quarterfinals, Sammy! And you didn't even want to come!"

"I was lucky," he said, without looking up from his spaghetti bolognese.

"You can say that again," Rudolf interrupted. "On the tatamis on the left, it's a much tougher competition. The people *you're* facing are lightweights compared to them — especially that one you were talking with at the beginning."

"Monk?"

"Could be. That guy's a real butcher. He wiped them all out in under a minute!"

"Is there any chance that you'll be facing him?" asked Grandma worriedly.

"I haven't looked at the lineup," Sam said evasively. "But I don't think I'll get very far this afternoon. Can I have some more spaghetti?"

Over dessert, Rudolf pulled Lily's cell phone from his pocket and put it on the table. He had an enigmatic expression on his face.

"I had a question for you, Sam. You didn't sell the phone, but you used it, right? You took some photos?"

Sam mentally cursed. Rudolf must have stuck his nose into the digital album! Good thing he had erased the spoiled pictures of the knights!

"Have you been snooping, Rudolf? Lily won't like that."

Rudolf slammed his napkin on the table. "You aren't planning to teach me manners, are you? How did you get those photos?"

"What are they pictures of?" Grandpa asked.

"An old city in the snow. In the *snow*, in this season: Can you believe it? I want to know where he took them."

"If that's all it is," Grandpa said with a sigh.

"Don't you realize what's going on?" asked Rudolf excitedly. "He's lied to us from the beginning! He wasn't at his father's place the other day! Nor at the train station last weekend! He's off wandering God knows where!"

For a second, Sam thought he'd been found out. Or had Lily told him? No, that was impossible. Rudolf just couldn't abide anyone standing up to him.

"There was a really great show on the cities of Europe on Thursday evening," said Sam. "Didn't you see it? I just took pictures of the TV screen."

"You're lying! The pictures couldn't be such good quality!"

"Oh, but this camera has very good definition," Sam said innocently. "Seven megapixels, right? Because you always pick the best, don't you? Now excuse me; I have to go warm up."

He stood up to cut off any extra interrogation. But when he entered the dojo, the competition was far from resuming. Many people were eating sandwiches in the stands, and groups of judokas stood around the tatamis.

"This is a big day for you!" said Pete Moret in a friendly way. "I've never seen you in such good shape."

"Thanks!"

"Do you know who you've drawn for the quarterfinals?"

"I . . . I'll go take a look."

Instead Sam first took a detour through the locker room, because he had seen Monk over by the computers, and he didn't feel like being subjected to another round of insults. Monk over by the computers. . . . The idea came into his mind while he was washing his hands. Monk over by the computers! But of course — how stupid he was!

He quickly pulled on his *gi* and rushed over to the officials' table. Cathy had told him Monk was a computer genius, but Sam hadn't realized he was actually running the computers for the tournament! He could easily have rigged the draw to let Sam win a number of bouts — by assigning him weaker opponents, for example. That would explain his string of successes this morning. And then Monk could be sure they would meet . . .

"Excuse me, do you have the lineup for the quarterfinals?"

Cathy handed him the sheet. "Good luck, Sam!"

Sam examined the boxes and arrows: *Quarterfinals A: Jerry Paxton vs. Sam Faulkner.* Whew! It wasn't Monk! Sam knew Jerry Paxton, who belonged to the Sainte-Mary team. He wasn't a monster, but he was well built and pretty tough, so there would be no shame in losing to him. Sam smiled to himself. He could defend himself weakly against Paxton and end the tournament unhurt and without embarrassment. At worst, if Paxton made a big mistake . . . Sam picked up the sheet again: *Quarterfinals B: James Farley vs. Michael Joly.* One of those two would be competing in the semifinals! Life was good, whatever might happen.

Sam looked for Paxton in the stands. The audience was filing back into the gymnasium to watch the end of the tournament, and many spectators milled around, waiting for their friends. Paxton might be hanging out with the older club members on the north seats.

Suddenly, Sam saw something that left him thunderstruck. Paxton was indeed over on the north side, but he was sitting away from the others, at the foot of the bleachers — with one arm wrapped around Alicia Todds.

Alicia Todds! *Sam's* Alicia Todds! *Alicia Todds was here!* And she was going out with Jerry Paxton . . .

Sam leaned against the scoreboard to keep from collapsing. Even at this distance, Alicia's beauty radiated through the gymnasium — *Yser's beauty,* Sam couldn't help thinking: the same pale skin and piercing eyes. She wore tight jeans and a black top that showed her stomach. Paxton was kissing her as eagerly as if they had just met, their hands intertwined. Sam felt like throwing up. *Alicia . . .*

He had to talk to her. This was probably the worst possible time, but he had to. They had a connection through time, a connection whose existence she couldn't even imagine, but which went beyond everything — even his embarrassment and fears. Yes, he had to talk to her.

In a daze, he made his way over to the north section and stood awkwardly in front of the couple, who were still kissing.

"Hello!"

They looked up at him in surprise.

"Faulkner?" Paxton said. "We haven't started again, have we?"

"No — that is . . ."

"Hi, Sam," Alicia said.

He couldn't speak.

"Sam and I have known each other for a long time," she

told Paxton composedly. "We used to be neighbors." She was looking at him with something indefinable in her eyes — interest, curiosity, resentment perhaps, and memories — so many memories! Sam jabbed his fingernails into his palms.

"You lived near Faulkner?" Paxton said. "You never told me that!"

"We haven't spoken for at least three years," Alicia answered. "I didn't know he'd come over to say hello. Unless it's only because of the fight?"

"I'm really sorry, Alicia," Sam stammered. "I . . . I've been so stupid. I should have come to see you, to explain. It was all so mixed up! . . . And you . . . you've changed!"

You're incredibly beautiful, he added to himself, *and you'd have to be blind not to see I still love you.*

"I suppose that's a compliment," Alicia said with amusement. "You've grown too."

Paxton was getting impatient. "Okay, Faulkner. We'll settle this later, all right? Go warm up with Moret. You're going to need it."

"Okay, of course, I'm bothering you . . ."

He backed away with the distinct feeling that he looked like an idiot. Alicia continued to look at him with that indefinable expression, and Paxton shot him a contemptuous smile, as if to say: *Clear out, loser! Alicia belongs to me!*

For Sam, letting himself be beaten was now out of the question.

CHAPTER NINETEEN

Hansoku-Make

The final rounds would take place on the central tatami. To warm up, Sam ran through a couple of workouts with Pete. From time to time he glanced over toward Alicia, but she had her back to him. She would have to look at him sooner or later.

"Sam Faulkner!"

He climbed up to the tatami amid applause and bowed to Paxton, who stood stiffly on his side of the mat.

"Hajime!"

The first clash was a rough one, as Sam and Paxton fought to grab the collar or sleeve of their respective *gi*s. Paxton achieved his grip first, but Sam had no intention of giving in. Six centuries earlier, he had helped Alicia Todds's ancestor get rid of the constable, and he wasn't about to look ridiculous in front of her descendant! Paxton seemed very sure of himself, and Sam hoped he could turn his overconfidence against him. The problem was that Paxton was a couple of inches taller, so Sam had to keep him at a distance. He tried a couple of attacks, though less in the hope of scoring points than to avoid being penalized for lack of combativeness.

Then in the third minute, when Sam was beginning to feel tired, Paxton gave him an opening. No doubt planning to use his size to his advantage, he caught Sam by the collar to pull him backward and put him off balance. But Sam wasted no time: He wrapped his shoulder under Paxton's arm, bent his knees in the same movement, and threw himself forward. Paxton's body traced a lovely curve through the air and crashed down on the mat. *Blam!*

"*Ippon!*" shouted the referee.

There was a thunder of applause. Sam had won! He stood up, not quite believing it. Grandma was blowing him kisses and Rudolf looked crestfallen — a double victory! In the north bleachers, Alicia was on her feet. Even though Paxton was her boyfriend, she was looking at Sam. . . .

Master Yuko was among the first to congratulate him. "What did I tell you, Sam? You shouldn't be afraid to trust yourself! You have what it takes to go all the way!"

Sam accepted the compliment without admitting that he planned to be flattened in the semifinals. At this point, he had held up his end of the deal!

In the next half hour, he distractedly watched three other fights. Ronald Joly won the quarterfinals B after fighting ferociously on the ground, while Monk qualified, to no one's surprise, at the expense of a black belt from Fontana. But neither match had the least importance to Sam, and it was with a completely free mind that he prepared to fight — and lose — his semifinal match.

Except that two minutes before the bout, Cathy came and tapped him on the shoulder.

"Hey, Sam! I've got great news for you. You're going straight to the finals!"

"What?"

"Michael Joly sprained his shoulder in the last round and had to forfeit. So you'll be in the finals!"

"What?"

"Is it that loud in here? You're in the finals!"

At the microphone, the announcer confirmed the cancellation of the bout and summoned the other semifinalists to the tatamis — in this case, Monk and the blond boy he was taunting at the start of the tournament. Sam was aghast. From his bench, he watched as they rushed at each other like savage beasts, colliding with hoarse shouts. At one point the tall blond boy tried to lift Monk off the mat. As he strained under the weight, Sam could distinctly hear his ribs crack — or his bones or joints, it wasn't quite clear. The attempt failed, and the two grappled all the harder. The referee even had to intervene to keep them from putting their eyes out.

Sam closed his eyes. *I'm facing Monk in the finals, in front of Alicia . . . I'm facing Monk in the finals, in front of Alicia . . .* When he opened his eyes again, Monk was on his back with his opponent trapped between his legs. He was squeezing him so tightly that the blond boy had turned almost purple. Finally the boy rapped several times on the ground to signal that he was giving up. The gymnasium exploded in cheers. Sam had only a few more minutes to live!

The fifteen minutes before the finals was especially awful. Everybody tried to encourage him or give him advice, while Sam just felt sick to his stomach. It was exactly as if he had used the stone statue . . . The statue! This was just the time when it would have come in handy! Why not take a little trip to Japan, at whatever time in history? But it was in his basement on Barenboim Street, and Sam was going to die here, in the Sainte-Mary gym, before the screaming crowd!

With dread, he took off his *zoris* and climbed to the mat. Three feet away, Monk looked even more impressive in his white *gi*, like some sort of abominable snowman, a miniature yeti — and a yeti who was licking his lips, to boot.

Monk was actually licking his lips! He planned to eat Sam raw!

The image was so infuriating that Sam felt a new burst of energy. He forced himself to concentrate: He was going to lose, perhaps, but he'd hold his head high. Grandma was there, and Alicia. . . . But the more he concentrated, the more a slight fog seemed to float before his eyes. Maybe his unconscious was keeping him from seeing. . . .

He had to hang on for just forty-three seconds to beat his record against Monk from last year. He could do that.

"Hajime!" the referee barked.

Monk leaped at Sam, who managed to hold his stance until the last moment, when the larger boy caught his sleeve and forced him to turn. The Monk-yeti reeked of sweat and smelly feet. He calmly stuck out his leg to test Sam on the right side, seeming to be in no hurry to finish him off. First he would tire him, play with him. . . . The old cat-and-mouse story! Monk casually launched a hip throw, and Sam was barely able to avoid it, twisting his wrist in the process. In his *gi*, Monk's huge, grotesque shape seemed unreal to him — unlike his breath, alas.

Then Sam realized that Monk was starting to repeat his

gestures again and again — like Lily when he met her in the basement, or like Paulus the lion cub on TV. Monk would stretch out his arm to grab Sam's *gi*, feint with his body to pull him toward him, and then stretch out his arm again and repeat the feint . . . It was so distracting that Sam didn't see the masterful sweep that sent him to the mat. He thudded to the ground and only avoided an *ippon* by landing on his butt instead of his back.

"*Waza-ari!*" the referee announced.

Seven points for Monk. Sam curled forward into a ball to avoid the big hands trying to push him on his back. If Monk really wanted to, he'd have no trouble finishing the match on the ground. But he clearly had a little more torture in mind first.

"*Matte!*"

The referee gestured to the opponents to separate, stand up, and adjust their *gi*s. There was no sound from the stands. Monk sauntered toward Sam, a slight smirk on the corner of his lips. Then he abruptly backed up and sauntered forward again, with the same ugly smirk at the corner of his lips. Sam blinked: The déjà-vu effect was now firmly established. But was he seeing Monk's moves *after* they happened, or *before* . . . ?

Sam nimbly shifted his ankle just as Monk tried to sweep it out from under him. It *was* before! He could anticipate his opponent's moves! When Monk bent down to grab Sam's legs — no doubt planning to lift him up, throw him over his shoulder, and earn a resounding *ippon* — Sam merely had to back up a few inches to foil the maneuver and unbalance his opponent. The yeti looked surprised, and a murmur went through the arena. What was happening?

Monk launched another hip throw to catch Sam on his side.

But Sam again anticipated it, and followed the move by working around Monk, even timidly attempting a sweep. Monk looked totally taken aback. Of course judo under these conditions wasn't very fair, Sam told himself. But what was fair in a fight between him and Monk?

Monk struggled to place his holds again and again, but Sam continued to defeat them, and sometimes even counterattacked. The fight was turning into a kind of dance, an unexpected ballet between David and Goliath. And Monk was getting angry, Sam could tell. Finally Monk launched one of his favorite moves, *morote*. If the move had gone properly, Monk would have stuck his bent forearm under Sam's armpit and turned his body, throwing Sam onto the mat. But Sam had already had a preview of the move, and at the very moment when Monk bent his arm for the pivot, he threw himself forward with all his might, carrying the bigger boy with him in his fall. Borne by his weight and momentum, Monk did a sort of rough cartwheel before falling heavily to the mat.

"*Waza-ari!*" exclaimed the referee.

A wave of astonishment went through the audience. The score stood at 7–7. Sam had managed to tie the match! He jumped to his feet quickly — he had everything to lose on the ground — and looked at the timer on the wall: thirty-eight seconds. He just had to hang on for thirty-eight more seconds, and the match would be over.

Monk stood up in turn, no longer even faintly in a good mood. Panting like an ox, he took just enough time to check his belt and rushed at Sam — twice! Leading with his arm, he tried to grab Sam by the sleeve, but the big hands closed on empty air. A few laughs rang out from the audience — including Alicia's, Sam could have sworn it!

"I'm going to crush you!" Monk screamed. "I'm going to —"

The referee stamped his foot.

"Hansoku-make!"

The two fighters froze. Everything in the gym seemed to stop as the referee pointed at Monk. It was forbidden to threaten one's opponent, and *hansoku-make* meant immediate disqualification for behavior contrary to the spirit of judo. Monk was eliminated! Sam had won the finals!

Then suddenly it was as if a tropical storm had hit the gymnasium. The audience was applauding so hard, the bleachers shook. Grandpa danced from side to side, giving Sam a thumbs-up victory sign; Grandma was shaking her head incredulously. The two finalists bowed to each other — Monk had his eyes lowered — and at Pete Moret's urging, Sam was carried in triumph around the hall. He made two laps, perched on a forest of shoulders and arms, everyone yelling, "Faulk-ner! Faulk-ner!" while he tried to spot Alicia. Finally he saw her, in a corner of the north bleachers, and it seemed to him that she was smiling.

After ten minutes of delirium and the official awarding of the medals, Sam finally escaped to the showers and some peace and quiet. He spent a very long time under the water until the echo had completely disappeared. *Stone statue, thank you! Time travels, thank you!* He would never have been able to outlast Monk without them! He would never have won the gold medal!

He walked into the locker room with a towel around his

waist, half expecting Monk to be waiting in front of his locker. But the room was empty. The yeti had disappeared! And yet someone was knocking on the little windows near the ceiling. Sam looked at the crouched silhouette behind the frosted glass. Was it possible that Alicia . . . he climbed up on the bench and turned the latch, his heart pounding.

"Lily?"

"Sammy, excuse me for . . ." She looked in through the window to make sure no one else was there. "Rudolf is in the parking lot with Grandpa and Grandma. I didn't want them to see me."

"Did you hear I won?" Sam said excitedly. "The gold medal! I beat Monk, can you believe it?"

"Yes, Pete told me. That's terrific!" But she barely smiled, and he noticed that she seemed pale.

"You look a little upset," he said cautiously.

"You remember that I went to the library this morning? That I had some books on reserve?"

"Yeah, so what?"

She loosened the strap on her bag and pulled out a book. "I was doing more research on Vlad Tepes, trying to get all the information I could."

"That's nice of you, but . . ."

She passed him a book through the window. "This one talks about one of his castles in Wallachia."

Sam took the book in his hands: *Bran, Dracula's Castle.* The cover showed a fortress on a rocky spur, with towers and fortifications.

"There are lots of photographs inside," she added. "Even a few shots of the dungeons. I put in a bookmark; take a look."

She said the last words in a tiny voice, and Sam quickly opened the book to the place she'd marked. The pictures showed a low room with stained walls and thick iron rings for balls and chains. Was this the place where Vlad Tepes had locked up his father? The illustration in the Book of Time had showed a castle like this.

"Look at the last picture on the right," Lily said in the same small voice. "It says the graffiti is from Vlad Tepes's time."

Sam brought the book closer. The picture showed a wall with a faint inscription crudely scratched into the stone. It took Sam a few seconds to make it out, since some of the letters were hard to read, but there could be no doubt about the author of the message. Six centuries earlier, in the depths of his cell, Allan Faulkner had scrawled:

HELP ME SAM

Turn the page for
these bonus features!

ABOUT THE AUTHOR

ABOUT THE TRANSLATOR

A CONVERSATION WITH
GUILLAUME PRÉVOST

DISCUSSION QUESTIONS

FUN FURTHER READING

A SNEAK PREVIEW OF
THE BOOK OF TIME II:
THE GATE OF DAYS

About the Author

Guillaume Prévost was born in Madagascar in 1964. He knew from the age of six that he wanted to be a writer, but hardly wrote anything until he was in his mid-twenties for fear that it wouldn't be very good. Instead, he studied literature and history. An alumnus of France's prestigious École Normale Supérieure, he teaches history at a school near Paris. After contributing to the *Histoire* television series and writing various specialized works, he turned to literature, producing a series of well-crafted adult historical detective novels, before writing *The Book of Time*. Prévost lives near Versailles, France.

About the Translator

William Rodarmor is an award-winning French translator, writer, and editor. In 1996 he received the Lewis Galantière Award from the American Translators Association for *Tamata and the Alliance* by Bernard Moitessier, and in 2001 he won for his American publisher the Batchelder Honor Award for his translation of the young adult novel *Ultimate Game* by Christian Lemann. His other young-adult translations include *The Last Giants* and *The Old Man Mad About Drawing*, both by François Place, and *Catherine Certitude* by Patrick Modiano. Rodarmor lives in Berkeley, California.

A Conversation with Guillaume Prévost

Interview conducted by Leslie Budnick
Translated by William Rodarmor

Q: The Book of Time *is your first book for younger readers.*
Why did you decide to write for this audience? What do you hope
kids will come away with after reading this book?

A: As a writer, I started with a couple of historical mysteries
"for adults." I found the writing very interesting but limited by
the rules of the genre (believable intrigue, police procedurals,
etc.). I felt like letting a big breath of fresh air blow over
my characters and giving free rein to my imagination while
keeping the historical context extremely accurate. To jump
from the trenches of World War I to the Ramses III royal
tomb workers in two chapters is an incredible luxury for an
author—a luxury that young adult literature has given me!
I hope that when young readers finish this book they will at
least think one thing: History is fascinating! Some of them
may even be curious enough to follow in Sam's tracks and
to go see where and in what eras he traveled. On occasion,
Sam turns to the Internet for more information; the reader
is invited to do the same.

Q: *What kind of research did you do in creating* The Book of
Time*? Are the people Sam encounters in his time travels real, as*
well as the locations and the historical events? Have you actually
traveled—in current time—to all the places Sam travels?

A: Beyond the book's adventure and suspense aspect, I was determined that the periods that Sam travels to would be as accurate as possible. Not just movie backdrops, but real moments of history. The illuminated manuscript that Sam manages to save from the Viking invasion (on the Island of Iona around 800 A.D.) really exists. Likewise, Corporal Chartrel, whom Sam helps during the battle of Verdun, really was wounded in the way I describe. The strike of the workers of Thebes that Sam joins actually happened. And each time these are central plot elements. Tightly linking history and fiction was at the heart of this project! As for actual research, I suppose I'm only doing my job, if not as a historian, at least as a history teacher. That's a job enriched by my own taste for traveling: I have thoroughly enjoyed wandering around Iona and Bruges, in particular.

Q: *As a history teacher, how do you engage your students? Are you able to bring history to life for your students in the same way that you do in* The Book of Time?

A: So far, the French national education system does not allow the stone statue to be used in class! But like all teachers, I feel there is a theatrical side to teaching and that the spoken word can be as evocative as the written one, even within a fairly structured program. When talking to my students I tried to stress the human side of history, to help them understand, for example, that the Greeks who invented democracy in Athens were in some ways different from us, but in many others, very similar. That's what makes them close to us, and important and useful to know: They still have things to tell us today. And that approach isn't so different from that of *The Book of Time*.

Q: *Is the stone statue based on an historical artifact, or is it purely of your imagination?*

A: It is not an accident that no one is allowed to enter my secret cave! Everything is there: the stone statue, the coins with holes, the Book of Time....Except that this cave is somewhere deep in my brain, so there is no danger I will lose the key to it. Seriously, though, one of the first things I had to do when I dreamed up this story was to take a piece of paper and sketch the stone statue, so as to fully understand its mechanism and its potential. Today I keep that drawing carefully hidden, because it has caused a lot of laughter from the people around me.

Q: *So often, aspiring writers are advised to write what they know. Are there elements in* The Book of Time *from your own life? And do you have any advice for young authors?*

A: There are certainly parts of the book that are taken from my own life. In particular I am lucky enough to have a son and a daughter who share some character traits with Sam and his cousin Lily. Also, like Sam, I have done some judo (without winning any major trophies, alas!) and I like video games, computer technology, rock and roll, etc. In other words, there is a part of me that is still fourteen years old. As for advice to young writers, I'm probably not the best person to give it. But I will say this: On a daily basis, I think writing is more a matter of willpower than talent. Pretty encouraging, don't you think?

Q: *The plot of* The Book of Time *is extremely intricate and the characters vivid. Can you share some of your influences as a writer? Where do your inspirations come from? Were you a reader as a child? What are some of the books you enjoyed reading? Do you think they influence your writing as an adult?*

A: I was very influenced by what I read when I was young. I was a big reader, because I never found any other activity that so deliciously took me out of the world while teaching me so much about it. Isn't the desire to dive into a book that you are reading one of the strongest of feelings? It was probably because of my desire to make that feeling last that I always wanted to be a writer. Among the authors who influenced me growing up, Jules Verne was the first to make me passionate about adventure. As an homage, I even made him the hero of one of my books (*Le mystère de la chambre obscure*). I also devoured a lot of mysteries, including the classics: Sir Arthur Conan Doyle, Agatha Christie, Maurice Leblanc, Gaston Leroux, etc., which clearly affected my way of building plots. Nothing should be accidental; everything should mean something. This has almost become a way of thinking, and my children now forbid me from saying anything when we're watching a mystery on TV or at the movies, because I tend to quickly spot the guilty party, his motive, and methods. A professional deformity, in some ways. Then, when I was thirteen or fourteen, I went through an intense science-fiction period: Isaac Asimov, A. E. Van

Vogt, Jack Vance, etc. That's related to my desire to invent stories that go beyond a purely rational framework. Add to this a precocious interest in history, and I would say that *The Book of Time* was probably mainly written to appeal to the child I once was.

Q: The Book of Time *was originally written in French. What role did you play in its translation? Did you work with William Rodarmor, the translator, directly, or through Scholastic, your American publisher? Can you tell us a little about the process?*

A: My grown-up novels have been translated into several languages, but my relationship with my translators was limited to a few e-mails to clear up some point or other. With William Rodarmor, all that changed! He started by telephoning me to introduce himself, and we very quickly built a relationship of trust. And he got passionately involved with the text, wanting to know everything about everything, including somewhat remote elements of the historical context that would better enable him to understand this or that detail. He literally bombarded me with messages and sometimes tracked me to my lair, because he wound up knowing the book better than I did! And all this with great good humor. In short, the translation was a novel and enriching experience, and it should continue with the next volumes. We then went over the final version with editor Cheryl Klein of Arthur A. Levine Books, and I was struck by her intelligent reading of the text. So I have been part of the translation process from beginning to end, which is a wonderful piece of luck for the writer, but also, I hope, for the book!

Q: *Lastly, can you give us any hints about what's to come for Sam, Lily, and Allan? We can't wait to read more about them!*

A: Hmm.... *The Gate of Days* has many revelations for Sam about his father and his family's story, and Lily may wind up more involved in her cousin's quest than she might like. And as in *The Book of Time*, I can promise you a real surprise at the end!

Discussion Points

Questions written by Leslie Budnick

Characters

1. Is Sam brave because he is willing to risk his own life in order to save his father, or is he a coward because he doesn't want to face Monk? Can a person be both brave and afraid?

2. Even though Sam's father is missing, there is no shortage of adults to care for Sam. Compare Aunt Evelyn and Rudolf as "parents" with Grandma and Grandpa. Who would you respect more? Why? How does Sam's behavior toward the four differ? How does Sam feel about his aunt and Rudolf's opinions of his father?

3. While Allan Faulkner has not appeared in the story yet, he *feels* very present. What stories and events have brought him to life?

4. Contrast Sam's and his grandparents' feelings toward Allan Faulkner with Aunt Evelyn's. Describe your impression of Allan Faulkner's personality, from his fingernail clipping collection to his Egyptian travels to how he rates as a dad and a businessman.

5. How does Sam's relationship with Lily change over the course of the novel?

6. Sam makes many references to his life prior to his mother's death three years ago. How have his life, his relationships, his schoolwork, and his environment changed in those three years? Has his life changed since his discovery of the stone statue? How?

7. The name Dracula conjures up many images and feelings for Sam and Lily, as well as for readers. But what is truth and what is fiction? Discuss what you think you *know* about Dracula. Make a list. Then look up Vlad Tepes and Dracula to see what is true and what is lore, and make a corresponding list. What new information was uncovered? What surprised you? What scared you?!

Setting

1. The author, also a history teacher, says, "When talking to my students I tried to stress the human side of history, to help them understand, for example, that the Greeks who invented democracy in Athens were in some ways different from us, but in many others, very similar. That's what makes them close to us, and important and useful to know: They still have things to tell us today." Pick one of Sam's destinations or intended destinations. What do you think its history still has to tell us? What knowledge can we gain from Sam's experience in that time?

2. Which of Sam's destinations was your favorite? Why? If you could travel in time where would you choose to go? If you couldn't choose your destination would you

still choose to travel? What if it were a matter of life and death—like saving your father?

3. The author was diligent in maintaining authentic and accurate backdrops to Sam's travels. List the places in Sam's travels. Choose one and find out more about the place and its people. Describe a difference and a similarity between it and your present location. As the author offers, "On occasion, Sam turns to the Internet for more information; the reader is invited to do the same." So do it!

Plot

1. The author has taken care to plant clues to foreshadow future events in the current story and in the future books of the trilogy. As the author says, "Nothing should be accidental; everything should mean something." Did you notice that Monk is called a "computer genius" in chapter 1? How does this affect the story later? What other clues/seeds can you identify? Discuss what each clue foreshadows and its significance, what it *means*, as well as what it might lead to.

2. Sam has learned that he needs special coins to activate the stone statue in order to travel. He's also discovered the key to being able to return home—the right coin plus someone thinking of him. What eludes him is how to choose his destination accurately. Discuss and hypothesize about how this aspect of the stone statue might work. Could it be related to the book or the

sunrays on the statue? Other ideas?

3. What makes Rudolf appear to be a suspicious character? Why might he be so interested in Sam? What could be his motives? Discuss how Rudolf might figure into the overall plot of the trilogy.

4. "Beyond the book's adventure and suspense aspect," says the author, "I was determined that the periods that Sam travels to would be as accurate as possible.... Tightly linking history and fiction was at the heart of this project!" Look at the settings, the characters, and Sam's research. What seems fictional and what factual? Then look it up for yourself. You might be surprised by the answer!

Theme

1. Heroism is a strong theme throughout the story and among the people Sam meets in his travels, as well as in Sam's own actions. What makes a hero? How is Peneb a hero? How is Yser a heroine? Is Friedrich a hero for risking his own life in order to help Sam? Who else might you consider a hero? Lily?

2. Lily helps translate the Latin that Sam finds in the constable's laboratory to read:

He who gathers the seven tokens will be the master of the sun. If he can make the six rays shine, his heart will be the key to time. He will then know the immortal heat.

Sam then interprets this text as:

Tokens = coins. U have 2 get 7 coins with holes in them 2 really make the statue work (=choose your time?). The 6 rays R those of the sun. How 2 make them shine? No idea. The sun must light up, maybe? The immortal heat…U burn but you dont die=heat+immortal. Well I guess. Tell me if thatz right according to U!

How else might this text be interpreted? Any ideas how to make the rays shine?

3. Right versus wrong is a strong theme throughout the story, and Sam is faced with many difficult decisions and ethical dilemmas. Was it ethical for Sam to use the cell-phone calculator in order to get the coin? Was it okay for Sam to divulge Van Eyck's secret ingredient to Baltus? Should Sam share what he knows about his father and the stone statue with his grandparents? Discuss Sam's motives and his reasoning behind these decisions. Identify additional ethical dilemmas that Sam and other characters face. Would you make different choices? Why?

4. Family loyalty is also an important theme throughout the book. This applies not only to Sam and Lily, but to many of the characters that Sam encounters. Cite examples of characters demonstrating family loyalty or breaking the bond.

Fun Further Reading

A String in the Harp by Nancy Bond
Baseball Card Adventures series by Dan Gutman
Both Sides of Time by Caroline Cooney
Chasing Vermeer by Blue Balliett
Dark Shade by Jane Louise Curry
The Devil's Arithmetic by Jane Yolen
Gregor the Overlander series by Suzanne Collins
Moon Window by Jane Louise Curry
Mr. Was by Pete Hautman
Out of Time by Caroline Cooney
Prisoner of Time by Caroline Cooney
Running Out of Time by Margaret Peterson Haddix
Something Upstairs by Avi
Time Cat by Lloyd Alexander
Time for Andrew by Mary Downing Hahn
Time Windows by Kathryn Reiss
Tom's Midnight Garden by Philippa Pearce
The Transall Saga by Gary Paulsen
The Window by Jeanette Ingold
The Wright 3 by Blue Balliett

The inside of the dinosaur's stomach reeked of epoxy and paint. Sam Faulkner crouched all the way in the back of the space, just where the body narrowed to a long fiberglass tail, and he was ready to move—to get out of not just the huge Baryonyx where he'd been hiding all evening, but out of the Sainte-Mary Museum. As soon as the guards completed their rounds, he would slip over to the coin room, take what he needed—Sam preferred to think of it as borrowing—and return to the dinosaur until the museum reopened in the morning. Then he would rescue his father.

He had never *wanted* to spend his nights hiding in a dinosaur's butt, Sam thought wryly. Indeed, if someone had told him two weeks before that he was going to steal from the museum—or that he would travel to ancient Egypt or World War I, or that his father was stuck in the fifteenth century as a prisoner of Dracula—he would never have believed them. But once you knew time travel was possible, and that a squat little stone statue in your basement could send you hurtling into the past, all sorts of possibilities—even necessities—opened up as well.

He tensed at the sound of footsteps in the hall. Two night watchmen switched on the light and walked by, a couple of feet from him, talking.

"The Baryo there isn't finished, either. Seems the painter won't come back till he's paid what he's owed."

"There's no more money for it," said the other man. "The curator says the city won't increase the subsidy. We need some new exhibits to bring people in. Did you read in the paper about that Greek thing they auctioned in London? The Navel of the World or some such? An old stone, and it went for ten million dollars in less than ten minutes! Our little museum can't afford that!"

"No kidding! Won't be long before they start firing people to cut costs!"

The guards were still grumbling as they crossed the hall to the far door and went out, leaving Sam alone again. He wolfed down two chocolate-nut bars he'd thought to buy from the vending machine and waited for the next round. The guards passed through again an hour and a quarter later, arguing about the merits of their favorite hockey teams. One was a staunch supporter of the Canadiens, the other swore by the Maple Leafs. Even though Sam felt that no one could match the Senators when they were on a roll, he was careful not to speak up. If the dinosaur suddenly gave its opinion on the Stanley Cup, the two men would surely have heart attacks.

Sam looked at his watch. It was past ten o'clock, and he had about fifty minutes to carry out his plan. In order to get the seven coins he would need to control his destination in time, Lily had suggested that he try the Sainte-Mary Museum, which held a number of bequests from Garry Barenboim, the strange old man who once owned the house that contained the stone statue. On a reconnaissance trip earlier that day, Sam learned that Barenboim had left the museum gold knives and forks, eighteenth-century hats, a mammoth tooth, a crystal goblet said to have belonged to the explorer Jacques Cartier, and an Aztec necklace—all things Sam suspected the man had gathered via time travel. He had also left five coins with holes in their centers, coins of just the right size.

And that was how Sam came to be crouching in a dinosaur's rear end at ten o'clock at night.

When he was sure the guards couldn't hear him, he left his hiding place and switched on his cell phone, finding his way by the screen's bluish light. Velociraptor to the right, triceratops to the left: All he had to do was head straight toward the front desk, going as far as the local history hall. The coin case was at the far end of the room.

Shrouded in darkness, the museum was as unnerving as a haunted house, with dozens of threatening shadows that seemed about to bite. *Come on,* Sam told himself, *there's nothing alive in here, just dusty old stuff.*

And yet…

When Sam opened the door to the hallway, he seemed to hear something like a key clinking against metal. He hid behind a statue of the sea god Neptune holding his pointed trident. Maybe one of the night watchmen had forgotten something. What to do? Going back was too risky, so Sam hunkered down, making himself as small as possible, and held his breath. There was a rustling noise on the floor, a flashlight beam in the next room, then nothing. Sam counted to a hundred before standing up. The coast was clear.

Hugging the walls, he reached the local history hall without any problem. There, the entire story of Sainte-Mary was told in large dioramas. Between each display stood costumed mannequins illustrating the town's different historical periods. As Sam walked toward a milkmaid emptying her pail, he saw a shadow moving about ten yards away, by the coin room. A dark shape was leaning over a display case and fiddling with something that made a slight squeaking. Sam slapped his cell phone against his thigh to hide the light, but it chose just that moment to ring—or rather to vibrate, because Sam had wisely switched off the guitar riff he used as a ringtone. Except that in the heavy silence of the local history room, it sounded as if one of the wax figures had switched on its electric razor!

The shadow whirled around, the beam from its flashlight catching the milkmaid's plump cheeks. Sam crouched behind her pail as best he could, but it was too late. The burglar— the *other* burglar!—was already rushing at him. The man raised his flashlight to hit Sam, who was just able to dodge the blow by rolling to the foot of a mannequin of Gordon Swift, Sainte-Mary's first and most venerable mayor.

Sam barely had time to stand up before the man was after him again, and a furious scuffle followed: He punched, Sam ducked, he tried to knee Sam, Sam twisted away, Sam kicked out, the man parried the blow easily. All this was done in total silence, so as not to alert the guards. The man was powerful, and apparently trained in this kind of hand-to-hand combat. He looked like a professional thief in a skintight black tracksuit, and he had taken the precaution of wearing a hood and gloves to hide his face and hands.

As Sam tried to grab him, he ripped the soft fabric of the burglar's tracksuit. The jerky light of the flashlight revealed a strange tattoo on his shoulder: a kind of U with flaring ends and a big circle between them. The man must not have liked having his clothes torn, because he began hitting harder. He even managed to slip his hands around Sam's neck, and gave a grunt of triumph as his thumbs started to crush his victim's Adam's apple.

With a sudden hip thrust he'd learned in judo, Sam knocked the man off balance, and the two of them tumbled into the legs of His Excellency Mayor Swift, who promptly toppled backwards with a crash of shattered glass. The museum alarm system started to howl and the hallway lights came on. The burglar scrambled to his feet, releasing Sam. Blinded and choking, Sam glimpsed the black, hooded shape briefly pause at the coin case before fleeing out the door beside it. Over the howling of the siren, he heard shouts.

"He's headed for the front desk! Hurry!"

The guards raced past the local history room without stopping, and Sam forced himself to stand up. There might be a chance to turn the situation to his advantage. He rushed to the coin collection. The display case housing the Barenboim bequest was wide open, its lock forced, but he swore as he took in the situation. All the coins with holes in them had disappeared, except one that the thief in black must have missed. There were two burglars after the same treasure!

"He's going for the service entrance!" cried a night watchman on the other side of the wall.

They'll be coming back, Sam told himself. *They're sure to come back.* They would search every nook and cranny of the museum, and the Baryonyx's belly wouldn't be much help to him. He had to leave now. But the only possible way out...

Sam glanced down the hall. Empty. He pocketed the last coin, crouched down, and ran in the opposite direction from the fugitive, keeping his ears cocked. The alarm had fallen silent, and he could hear muffled voices. When he reached the front desk, he looked in every direction. The service entrance was over by the locker rooms. It opened onto a dark hallway, and he could feel a breeze: the exit!

Outside, the guards were yelling, "Stop, thief! The museum's been robbed!"

As Sam felt his way down the hall, he bumped against a door handle on the right-hand wall and turned it. From the smell, it was a room where garbage cans were stored. He leaped inside, knocking over a broom cart, and yanked the door shut. His heart was pounding, and the rest of his body felt as if a train had run over him.

After a few minutes, the guards came back. They hadn't been able to catch the man in black.

"I'll...I'll call the police," gasped one, out of breath. "You try to see what he stole."

They walked down the hall without showing any interest in the brooms. Sam slipped silently out of his hiding place and quickly covered the last yards separating him from freedom. Fresh air! He ran down a small stone step, raced across a grassy rise, and sprinted to the corner without turning around. Taking streets at random, he didn't stop running until he'd put several blocks between himself and the museum.

It was only then that he realized he no longer had his cell phone.